Among the Fallen

VIRGINIA FRANCES SCHWARTZ

HOLIDAY HOUSE   NEW YORK

•• ● ••

First Edition
1 3 5 7 9 10 8 6 4 2

Library of Congress Cataloging-in-Publication Data

Names: Schwartz, Virginia Frances, author.
Title: Among the fallen / by Virginia Frances Schwartz.
Description: First edition. | [New York]: Holiday House, 2019. | Summary:
In Victorian England, sixteen-year-old Orpha, imprisoned for crimes she did
not commit, is released upon accepting the invitation of Charles Dickens
for a fresh start at a home for fallen women.
Identifiers: LCCN 2019005696 | ISBN 9780823441020 (hardback)
Subjects: | CYAC: Group homes—Fiction. | Secrets—Fiction. | Dickens,
Charles, 1812–1870—Fiction. | Sexual abuse—Fiction. | Orphans—Fiction.
Great Britain—History—Victoria, 1837–1901—Fiction.
Classification: LCC PZ7.S4114 Amo 2019 | DDC [Fic]—dc23
LC record available at https://lccn.loc.gov/2019005696

·· ● ··

FOR JEAN TONSKI
FROM ACROSS TWO CITIES
AND TWO COUNTRIES

·· ● ··

This work of historical fiction is set in England's Victorian era, where an insurmountable gap loomed between the rich and poor. While the wealthy few were waited on by servants, lived in mansions, and had plenty of food, the majority of the population in cities like London endured extreme poverty in overcrowded slums, faced hunger and starvation, and deadly cholera from drinking out of the Thames. Most people had no health care, sewers, or education. Child labor for children as young as nine and mass incarceration for petty crimes were common.

In this milieu, Charles Dickens began writing first as Boz and then used his real name. His novels shot arrows of social criticism that revealed the plight of London's lower class, featuring for the first time as main characters child laborers, members of street gangs, prostitutes, prisoners, thieves, and those condemned to workhouses for debt. Dickens's characters became household names: Fagin, Little Dorrit, Nancy, Scrooge, Tiny Tim, Pip, Magwitch, Jo the street-sweeper, and Oliver Twist. Dickens's novels shocked the isolated upper classes. Thanks to his work and that of influential philanthropists such as Lady Angela Georgina Burdett-Coutts, politicians finally began to address social ills—establishing the first sewers, a clean water system, vaccinations, the first public library, workday limits, some restrictions on child labor, prison reform, aid for abandoned children, housing developments for the working class, and free education for all children.

Settings integral to this novel, like Tothill, an infamous prison housing young adults, and Urania, a home for homeless girls supervised by Dickens and founded and funded by Lady Burdett-Coutts, were both in existence during this period.

In homage to Dickens, this novel is written in twenty sections to mimic the format of his own novels that appeared in twenty monthly installments issued in magazines. In those small glimpses, the wounded underbelly of Victorian society was sliced wide open for all to see. The public roared for more. Dickens was the most popular author of his time and continues to be admired to the present day by both readers and writers.

*My feet stop on the stone floor. I've been circling the cell round
and round. Eight steps ahead, then a turn to the left. Six steps
broad. Then eight once more. This is the path of worn grooves
my thin-bottomed boots pressed down upon when I first came
here.*

*I am caught up in him again like a web. But Luther is
free to come and go and torment me.*

*My fingers roam my face, a fallow field. Bony cheekbones.
Pointed chin. High forehead. Hollows for cheeks. Was there
ever a girl called Orpha, once?*

Tell me.

·· ONE ··

At the barred window—a slit in the brick, so high up one sees only sky—day begins as it does each and every morning, shifting from black to slate. A few moments are mine before the others awaken. Stealing time is one crime they cannot charge me with. "The sweetest sin is the one unseen," Hester hissed in my ear.

The hammock swings back and forth, as even as breath. My eyes are squeezed shut as I slip into the past perfect of another day. Bit by bit, I hear Pa again. It's always his voice that comes first, then his brown eyes. He had a voice that echoed everywhere, across the filled theater, booming along Old Pye Street, calling in passersby for the night's performance in the rookery, the slum we called home.

Creaks down Tothill's cold hallway. Flutter on the stairs.

Lemon balm leaves scent the air, picked in our back garden behind the theater, its pungent oil releasing into boiled water.

Gunfire pulses through these stone prison walls: 6:00 a.m. wake-up call.

Feet pound to the floor, and I am at the sink splashing icy water for my stand-up wash.

Hurry!

The cell must be tidied, hammock hung to the side, granite-gray uniform donned with the Red Star sewn on, white apron ironed down by palms, chamber pot in hand. My face flat as a plate.

We must be ready when they come.

The iron maidens are here. We curse Tothill's matrons with that name. Crisp black dresses like mourning outfits and that hard boot slam of theirs. Such a boot could kick a girl anytime. Foster, the tall eagle-eyed one, flips open the eyelet on my cell door, then slides the bolts, flinging the heavy door wide. She scans my dress and clipped hair tucked beneath a wide white bonnet.

"Get in line, E22!" she shouts, satisfied with my uniform.

Out of the next cell, E21, steps Ivy, neck bowed, a stray black curl peeking out of her cap. She is like a magnet: a girl to watch and wonder about; someone who pulls my thoughts outward. Her lips silently form an *O* in greeting while mine stretch into an *I*. We're quick at it, signals flashing fast, gone the next moment. It's enough to draw me into the line, into the day, to follow her. Then, one by one, we dump our chamber pots into slop buckets in the far hall and return them to our cells.

Afterward, I queue up behind Ivy. Every detail of her back I have memorized. Her shoulders slope more each day.

We've come to a juvenile prison for those under seventeen years of age. Young boys are housed here too, but we never see them or hear them, for they are kept in other wings. It's better that way. Most of us are here because of what boys turn into.

Fifty girls in E wing stand behind one another in order of their cell numbers, the doughy Matron Doyle at the head and the other matrons at the rear as if herding a flock of young turkeys to the chopping block. Doyle's broad shoulders and thick hands eager to grasp, marring us with bruises, are enough to keep us all looking straight ahead. Out in the open hallway, from every landing suspended above and below, eyes drill down on us; male guards on balconies, aware of every sniffle, a hand drifting from someone's side, or a misstep.

Up ahead, there's a stir. Rose is ordered to step out of line. Ivy too! Her eyes dart to mine, making my heart jump. Both join a group of girls and wait. Some girls I know only by face, not by name. All wide-eyed and stunned, not knowing where to look. Edwina's with them too, sniffling.

"E22!" Foster yells at me now. "Step out!"

My heart hammers a sore spot in my chest.

Stay invisible! Never show your inside on your outside. Where was it you learned that? First the workhouse, then your aunt's. Your own body betraying you: at twelve, buds of breasts poking through, making him see.

No one can save me from what's about to happen.

No one ever did.

Pa! Didn't I call you each and every time? My muffled words beneath Luther's fist: *Pa! Where are you?*

Girls from E wing join the other wings parading down to work in the oakum room, laundry, or kitchen. In our small group, the Red Star gleams on every arm, a badge of good behavior.

Ahead, Ivy shakes her head to signal a warning: *Keep in step. Don't falter.* No matter what's coming, punishment or lecture, at least we'll be together.

We march in a line of frayed girls upstairs to the very top. There is only one thing up there: the governor. He sits above us all. Matrons flank our backs as we are escorted into his office.

In his room of windows, Governor Tracey beckons us closer. A ring of girls surrounds his desk, Red Stars glaring.

"You are all nearing the end of your terms here in the coming months. Do any of you have a plan after discharge? Speak up now."

"My mum, Governor," Rose slurs in an odd voice

as she curtsies. "She's old and waiting on me to come home."

Ivy pipes up. "My man's promised to marry me once I'm out."

The governor scans the rest of us. One by one, we shake our dropped heads, eyes on our boots.

"Well, good, some of you are looking ahead. One thing I do not wish to see: any of you back at Tothill. Our records show that if you return to the same habits that brought you here, it is certain you'll return within the year."

My breath draws in very sharp. *I cannot return to the rookery, sir.*

"There is something else I'd like you to consider—"

Every eye lands on him.

"It's a home for fallen girls called Urania, where you will live with other girls for a year and be taught how to manage a household. Afterward, you will be transported to a position in one of the colonies."

None of us moves or says one word.

"If you are interested in being considered, tell a matron, and you will be interviewed. Placements may open up later as well. But first, you must have a physical examination to ensure you are a healthy candidate."

They'll want virgins.

Ivy doesn't even blink. Rose blushes. Edwina clenches

her hands. How awful she looks up close: swollen knuckles, half-eaten nails, and odd bumps all over her skin.

"Since most Tothill girls do not know their alphabet, I'll read this invitation aloud." He lowers his eyes to the letter. "You will all receive your own copy later."

As he reads, the matrons stiffen to attention. Foster glares at us as if we were bedbugs to be crushed. Her greasy black hair is flattened into a tight bun. She's bone and stone, as if someone carved all her fat away. Leaning away from the iron maidens, we girls circle the governor. His voice is slower than my heartbeat. My mind skips over the letter like a pebble skimming water so I only catch details here and there. One description about Urania floats like a sigh right into me: *refuge*. How odd. Girls kept apart and hidden. Just like now. Only this word sounds forgiving.

·· • ··

It's straight down to the oakum factory after that. The room is long and low with tall windows down the sides for natural light, but it is always silent and gray come winter. There is a fire, though, in the open fire pit, and it crackles. Oakum: old ship ropes; hemp to be tugged into thin fibers by raw hands; later, at the docks, coated with pitch to plug holes in seagoing ships. The day's allotments have already been weighed as we pass by to pick up our baskets. Girl after girl plops onto an assigned stool with a basket at her feet, pulling ropes onto laps.

Up front, on her high stool, Harred reigns like a queen over her sorry subjects. Narrow eyes in her flat face study our hands. Mostly she is silent. The only time she speaks is when she calls out a girl's cell number. Voices shout that number upon our chests if fingers aren't threading through the oakum quick enough. Behind us, through the narrow aisles, the other matrons patrol. It's impossible to know when one is right behind you, for they have learned to step stealthily upon the stone floor. Foster can scream in a girl's ear at any time. Without a word, Harred immediately scratches an *X* beside a cell number in her log should there be any disturbance.

This room is the one place where an inmate sits so close to the others, she can hear the sharp intake of air when oakum slices into an open cut or that breathless turn into silence when a girl daydreams herself away. Ivy works beside me. Her eyes shift from her lap to the aisles, up and down, waiting for the chance. When the matrons are all safely pacing with their backs turned, her hand slides to mine and lightly squeezes. Often she catches me drifting or silently cursing my cuts, calling me back into the room. She knows my every shifting mood.

I don't imagine it. Her touch whispers: *You're not what they say you are. You're not what they said you did. You're more.*

Girls upon girls in this factory. One hundred and seventy, I count today. Only the crown debtors come and go quickly.

Opposite are the youngest girls, from seven years to twelve, sneaks having snatched a bun from a cart, an umbrella by a door, or a piece of fruit. Their one mistake was not running away fast enough. They'll bolt quicker as they grow. Most pick their share of oakum, a pound's weight, once they're here some weeks. They'll go home soon after that. Since last spring, when I turned sixteen, my daily lot is a pound and a half of oakum.

Squinting, I unwind the lump of oakum into smaller strands whose sharp slices of tar prick the skin. These strands are then broken apart, one by one, unraveling the rope into thinner and thinner strands of strings. I roll them out flat on my thigh to loosen before fraying them against one another into ever-finer threads. The pile on my lap soon topples, sliding to the floor to join the mountain of picked oakum there. Before the pile is calf-high, my stomach rumbles like a thunderstorm.

Dare I look at the Red Star girls? Dare I tease out from their eyes what they are thinking about the letter? Dare I look to them for a sign? Best not to even think on it yet. Hester will return soon. Then we can decide.

A smoky smell haunts the factory from the dampened

fire that nobody bothers to tend now. It sinks down our noses as we breathe. Though we keep our mouths shut tight, the taste of tar coats our throats.

·· ● ··

At last, bells ring and we line up for breakfast. Skilly, a thin gruel like drips of snot. A hard half-quarter of toke, a bread so dry we cannot chew it, for most are missing all their back teeth. Cocoa sweetened with molasses for inmates with the yellow number 1 stitched on their arm, like those of us in E wing, first-class prisoners held from three months to three years. Only water with their meal for short-stay crown debtors. Their stares track us carrying our tin mugs to our stools, steaming the room. If you shut your eyes when you dunk the toke into it, you can pretend to be at a cart such as those I once passed in Covent Garden, its heat warming places grown cold overnight. In eight dips, the bread is gone.

The break is almost over. I allow my eyes to slide Ivy's way. Can your eyes read another girl like a book? Mine do. Today, she immediately catches my eye when my head turns. Her eyes smile back though her lips dare not. At once, it warms me. Her movements always speak for her. She sometimes stomps across the yard with no hesitation. She likes to have her own way, I suppose. In chapel, she's whispered how she spent lots of money on woolen stockings and hooped skirts of bright colors.

Those were the days, Orpha! I felt so fine! So flush! She pretended to be someone else before, as if her own self wasn't good enough. But lately, those tight cords in her neck and her head dropping. She has a weight pressing on her, and my hands wish to touch her there on her shoulder to lift it but cannot.

·· • ··

At nine fifteen, we are corralled into chapel, a kind of theater of ascending rows, each one higher than the next, facing the chaplain. Girls pack into separate cubicles like matchsticks inside a tin box. Wooden walls slam behind us and between us so we cannot see one another. It is like sitting in one's own coffin.

In this holy place, they think they have captured us. We mumble our morning prayers in a drone. Matrons patrol with hawk eyes. Dare we not look straight ahead, dare we not recite our prayers loudly enough, dare we cough or clear our dry throats, our names will be shouted out for punishment. Down to the crank then.

"You must be silent; you must be kept separate," Head Matron Harred lectures us with her forefinger pointing straight at us. "That's the law at Tothill!"

One sharp look from her and all the matrons scramble like chickens, stumbling over their own feet to get at anyone not paying attention.

All the while, the chaplain's beady eyes study us from

his high seat as if we were abominations. His prayers spit. His greasy hair pokes up on end as he raves on and on.

"All of you will be doomed to Hell's scorching fire if you don't confess to God!" he shouts at us. "Down on your knees this moment to ask His forgiveness upon your heathen souls!"

No one drops to her knees here. The others would slice her down with a glance if she did. To end, we sing a hymn. Today it is "Nearer My God to Thee."

Though like the wanderer, the sun gone down,
Darkness be over me, my rest a stone;
Yet in my dreams I'd be
Nearer, my God, to thee!

Some of us scream, for this is the only chance we get to open our mouths. So clever, this, as it covers the other voices traveling from girl to girl between the cubicles. Harred's glance cuts in all directions like a fox on a rabbit run. But there is such a din of voices no matron guesses whose mouth the words are spilling from. All mouths seem to be singing. Only we know, for we are inside the noise.

When Ivy raps on the wooden wall between us, I lean my ear against it to listen. The hollow wood is like a magic flute. Through it, her voice echoes. Only since last month do I dare answer back, ever watchful of Harred.

"Jack!" she cries. "He's not showed these last six months."

"He'll come!"

"What if he's found another?" she calls again.

I could spit at that. She's here because of him. And he is free to do what he likes. Just like Luther.

I shout back with all my might. "What will you do about the letter?"

No answer returns.

If we could go to the Home, we'd be safe from the streets, away from both Jack and Luther. But she doesn't see it the way I do. Of that, I am certain.

I knock again. But Ivy is elsewhere.

·· ● ··

Back to the oakum again until rope-walk. Children under ten years leave for the schoolroom. Those left behind don't budge, just stare into space, and soon their small heads bob till nudged. Mothers who birthed here visit their own babies in the nursery, the one place they must hear laughter and the sound of their own voices. I imagine that room ringing bright as Westminster's bells. As for the rest of us, we'll be wrapped in oakum, lost for hours.

·· ● ··

At last it is afternoon, three o'clock, the hour our heads drop.

"Forward for your exercise!" shouts Doyle. "Off your arse, girls! Step lively now."

We head out to the airing yard in circles of girls joined hand to hand by ropes to keep us all moving at the same even pace. They believe the rope-walk keeps us fit. We call it Devil's Circle.

Today Governor Tracey himself joins Harred and the other matrons, leaning their heads together, whispering near the prison wall, out of the wind, Foster's thin lips spilling foulness. They turn to stare boldly at our parade, pointing out Ivy.

Let her be! She's a Red Star girl. She's done nothing wrong here. In a second, they could pull her out, away from me, with one of Foster's lies. There'd be no way to protect her.

Hester finally joins us today. She's been in confinement in the darks, shut in the basement with the crank, a punishment tool that must be turned a certain number of rotations each day. She made the mistake of talking back to a matron.

Hester's the oldest girl here. She's a nightwalker. They say she lures men down into underground tunnels. That's how she makes money. Every matron knows her by name. She is here this time, she says, "'Cause the bribe I gave those constables wasn't enough so's they turned me in. The judge would hear none of that story. Fined me even more for being sassy enough to say so to the court. I couldn't pay up. But I wasn't lyin' one bit!"

These last five days, whenever we passed into the yard for our exercise, we could hear the crank squeaking round and round in regular rhythm. Whenever someone is punished, matrons are sure to lead us past the basement as warning of a life churning away.

Hester slides quickly into line now. Twists of black hair poke out of her cap like live hornets and venom twists her thin lips trying to jump out. Most girls hang on her words. She has survived both here and on the streets. Way out in front, at the turn, she lifts her hand to shield her mouth and tosses words to the wind in a voice thrown from the back of her throat. I lean my whole body toward her.

"Damn them! Five days in the dark of—"

We must wait until the next turn to hear the rest.

"—bread and water. Shoulder hurts awful and they—"

Harred's head turns. She sniffs the cold air. Her eyes bounce from girl to girl. Immediately, I tug hard on the rope. The human chain in front of me yanks upon their rope until Edwina, just behind Hester, pulls so hard Hester feels our warning throttle in her own hands. She slams her mouth flat.

"That you I hear, E29?" the Head Matron shouts across the yard, pointing to Hester. "Miss the churning, do you? One more word and it's back to the crank. Keep in step, all of you!"

We push round and round until we are all sweaty and flushed, the way they like. They lecture that quick walks open the lungs wide and aid our stomachs to digest. "Can't afford to dose you all with castor oil or bother the busy doctor," we've been told.

"Double quick!" Harred orders from the far wall.

Usually, all she does is point a finger and we quicken our steps. She rarely moves from her post. Beside her, the tall pink-skinned governor nods approval.

So we run in circles gasping until we hear, "Regular time!"

Up ahead, Edwina's right leg trails behind, slowing the whole line. You can tell where she is at once. She's always sniffling. Gray she is, stick thin, with no breasts at all, and a flattened nose.

"Get a move on there, E30!" Doyle shouts, heading closer.

And Edwina does. She scoots her thin body ahead, out of Doyle's reach.

"Two and a half years *gone*," Ivy whispers, brushing past as we go back inside the prison. "Seven months to go! I will never find myself again."

I catch the sign: her fingers trailing along the bricked wall. A signal between us: grief as hard as this stone. *Don't make me go back in there again*, it says.

This time, I take the chance. Pretending to stumble, I touch my hand to the small of Ivy's back to steady myself, pressing my warmth into her. Doyle shouts too late. For I have already changed Ivy. Her chin lifts, not hiding her grin.

Inside, girl after girl passes by, steering straight toward her pile of oakum like a ship toward land, sinking down upon her stool like a heavy anchor. A horrid odor fills the air in their wake: blood and rot. One of them must have her monthlies.

·· ● ··

The letter waits on the floor of my cell after we return from supper. Out of the corner of my eye, I see letters in the other cells too: one in Ivy's; one in Rose's, Edwina's, another in—there's that stench along the corridor again. Perhaps a poisoned rat hides dead in the walls. The door bolts behind me. And I am alone with something I dare not touch. It seems so alive and fresh.

But I do. Press its smooth surface to my face. It speaks to a girl called *you*. Immediately I draw to attention. Only to find it's an anonymous letter by someone who signs, *Your friend*. The tone is sweet and full of promises. It invites us when our term is up to enter a Home and change our lives. And not to go the round of most inmates—those who step out prison gates only to reenter them like a revolving door and grow old behind bars, without family or friends.

It ends with these words: "What you might have been, and what you are, oh think of it then, and consider what you might be yet!"

How did this writer know that I was once an innocent girl...even promising...I would have been an actress, like my mother, tutored by my own father, who tuned my voice to vibrate as a violin string does. But there isn't a house in the whole of London that would welcome me now.

In fifty days, I will be released. There are only certain places a Tothill girl can go. A girl's shaved crop and blackened palms marked by the scars of oakum picking tell a story. No one will befriend such a girl or offer her a post. People will gossip about what she may have done.

Pray Emma doesn't know, my one bosom friend from the rookery. This winter, she sent an inquiry to Tothill about me. But I did not answer her. Just my appearance and list of my crimes would make her cry. Let her think I am not here at all.

Soon I am spinning a path over the stone again. The thing to do is never stop. When my feet walk ahead, time runs away. There is no past or future then. Round and round I pace, though my stomach threatens to heave the grease from our dinner barley soup. It was supposed to be beef, but E37 cooks in the kitchen and let it be known on the rope-walk that rotting fly-ridden horsemeat was delivered yesterday.

This letter is a trap. From a man, most likely. No one could write like that except one, sweetening his words like a peppermint humbug one would bait a child with. But we are knowing here. No man writes a letter to ones such as us unless he wants something.

·· • ··

That night, after the nine o'clock blast of gunfire, in pitch dark, we push our mouths flat to the eyelet as the matron's bootsteps fade away at the end of her shift. There's thirty minutes before the next matron shows.

One voice, then others, echo in a chorus, "The letter! Did you get it?"

We shush. Wait for one voice to penetrate the corridor. Then press an ear to the eyelet so one's whole body becomes a listening vehicle. Edwina is a yeller. She calls out, wondering about the Home with the odd name: Urania. There's a tumble of voices again.

Hester taps us quiet. Her taps are the hardest. Likely her heel.

"Fools!" Her voice slams. "It's an asylum, *not* a refuge. More rules than here. Preachers and lashes. Hiding you away. Just like prison. Worse! Never let you out for air in case you sneak off!"

Her words blast at the eyelet. We hold still.

"I got nowhere else to go!" cries Edwina.

"It's a nunnery!" shouts a faraway voice. "I hear you must confess your crime and work every minute. If you don't—"

"You'll be dragged to the punishment room!" screams another.

Another yells, "It'll be the cat-o'-nine-tails licking your back then!"

"I was put in one at twelve!" Hester taps. "Bible reading all day long. Caned me if I complained about the hard work. So I ran away."

It sounds harsher than the workhouse where I was sent to pay Pa's debt. How could it be any worse than here, where we see nobody? Hester always has a say. But she was not called down. No letter waited on her floor.

·· T W O ··

I have a name but no one has ever said it aloud except Ivy. She called it across the dark corridor the night I arrived: "Orpha!" How odd to hear that name when all their charges still shouted in my ears, after they assigned me a number, confiscated my clothes, and swore I had no name anymore.

Where had she heard it? And did she know the worst of the charges?

Still she called my name aloud, risking punishment, brightening the dark. The whole of London had condemned me: constables, the doctor, nurses, the magistrate and the matrons. She did not.

Next morning, stepping out of the cell beside mine, she stood between the stone prison and me like a shield. Tiny. Half starved. Yet she looked wiry, slippery as a fish, as if she could somehow slide between these walls. As if she could teach me how to breathe here. But it was her eyes that made me wish to know her: big as coat buttons, and deep brown, just like Pa's. Those eyes darkened soon as she saw me, riveting to mine like she'd lost everything, wanting me to feel it too. I did. At once.

Promises shivered in the air between us as if she had spoken them: *You are not alone. We are here together. I have endured. You will too.*

Shadows already fall across the factory room when we come inside from exercise that afternoon. Oakum is heaped upon the floor by our stools. The tar's fumes cut deeper now after we've filled our lungs with frosty air. We bow our heads, as if praying. In the stillness, my head droops. Drafts needle my back. The air clots with fibers from fraying ropes and then the coughing starts. Dry hacking. Throat clearing. My nails throb again, split below the nail beds. Tar clings stickily to whatever I touch. There's no use scrubbing it.

My thoughts become a flat line. I will myself away. Floating above the oakum room, fingers still plucking. Another me looks down. All I see are Tothill's girls. Stalled before womanhood. Lips downturned. Eyes narrowed like cats cornered in alleyways. Backs raised. Tails, if they had them, curled beneath their bellies. Quick to hiss or curse.

I have become one of them: fallen.

When you are condemned for violence such as you believed you could never be part of, and all accusers point fingers at you, you look at yourself differently. The nurses' eyes that landed on me in my hospital bed refused to look away. The testimony of witnesses in the street where the women invited me in. The judge without mercy. My father's sister, Aunt Agatha, once a singer, and her husband, who both disowned me for being in that condition. She was the one who kicked me into the street, leaving me with no choice.

"Streets lust for girls to be thrown to them like live bait," Hester swears.

Suddenly I am no longer myself but who they say I am: a criminal; a common tart not to be trusted. Guilty. All I remember is falling in the street that day and how that changed everything. I never guessed what could happen to a girl. Either before or after.

Back and forth I toss that doomed time in my mind like a sizzling-hot chestnut. The year Luther owned me, body and soul. The accuser whose wallet was cleverly lifted. The day they caught me. If I did what they accuse me of—any of it—I have lost my own self.

I awaken with a jerk to oakum piled on my lap and the stern eye of Harred. My fingers know to hop double-time.

·· ● ··

After a supper of gruel and bread, heading upstairs in line to the dim cell on the north side of Tothill, I crave a peek outside at the quick fading light of a winter's dusk. Even on the grayest day, the deepest blue can gather around the pink edges of sunset, making the sky blush with promise. I get a glimpse of it now as we enter the main hall to march upstairs. By the time we step into E wing, it's become black night.

There's that stench in the air just now. It's one of us in E wing.

·· ● ··

On Sunday, there is no work after early chapel. No heat either. Hours alone in our cells.

"Silence will do its work on the lot of you," the chaplain lectures. "It will force you to face your sins alone and beg forgiveness."

Drafts blow through the seams in my thin boots, making my toes cramp. It helps to pace. It heats the core where your empty belly is. You can tramp down all you wish to forget. You can hold your mind still on what you like. I've waited long enough to do it.

Urania, the anonymous letter writer called it, a fancy name making me think of stars. Why? Hester called it an asylum but the letter said it was a refuge. One of them is lying.

There will be a family of girls there. I haven't had a real home since I was eleven. That's when Pa left. An orphaned girl doesn't get a family one, two, three. What price will I have to pay for it?

Ivy has a visitor today and is called down. Not once have I had one. Two visits a year, we are allowed. I bet it's finally Jack, her smasher, that forger: the one who made up the soft banknotes she passed. The one the constables could not find to bring to court. He's free. She's not. Why does she still love him, then? He's the reason she's here so long. She couldn't get enough of his money; can't get enough of him, even now. I imagine her skirts rustling as she scurries along the stone floor to him like a mouse out of its hole.

Later, to watch her walk to chapel with her head held high is to know for sure Jack's come with all kinds of sweet promises. She won't speak of them, holding them in her mouth like a Communion host.

On the other side of the cubicle, E41 bangs on the wood during hymns. "I hear they make slaves of you in those asylums. 'Cause you have sinned. All the Our Fathers in the world won't save you from the birch cane!"

After chapel, as Ivy files past, she catches the tip of my baby finger, leaving a trail of something warm and creamy. Inside my cell, I lift it to my nose. Lavender lotion! Light and floral, hinting of gardens and sunshine. Immediately, I press it into the ragged hangnail on my thumb.

To think that Ivy hid this lotion in her palm and slipped it to me, straight from her lover's hand into mine. Three feet of stone between us so we cannot rap or call one another. She thinks of me too.

·· • ··

It's Sunday evening. The young weekend matron Ayre arrives. Her uniform is not crisp like the others. Her blouse loosens at her thin waist as if she's hurried here. I don't think she lives at Tothill. Bet she has a home. Bet she has a mother.

If the week on our wing has been without incident, her first task is to leave all the eyelets open. Rose's cell door is ajar, so we can hear her singing as we read and rest in our cells. The matrons believe it essential to bathe our blackened souls with Christian hymns.

All along the E corridor, I imagine the other girls pressing their ears against cell doors as darkness falls too soon at the day's end. For the voice of an angel trails through the empty hallways:

When I from death shall wake,
I may of endless light partake.

Those singular notes vibrate in my chest until I become something other than I am. Can a girl fly invisible on wings and leave her own self behind? I do. For a time.

·· ● ··

Before entering her cell tonight, Ivy fills her lungs deep as if swallowing bad medicine. Hours ahead alone within stone walls when she just saw Jack. I want to catch her hand and let my touch linger on her skin as her lotion did on mine.

For Ivy, there's just Jack. She won't rest until she's with him.

I'll be out before her, in less than two months, if I toe the line. There's nothing I want like she does. Only to survive. And not get trapped ever again. But where could that place be without her?

·· • ··

Between what's real and what's imagined, there can be too thin a line. Sometimes I hear Luther's voice. Don't deny it. I cover my ears but he shouts anyway:

"Don't think of running. Or ever telling. Don't I know every inch of this rookery? Not a corner to hide in. I'll come for you. When I do, it'll be with this"—he swivels the Valentin knife until it glints in the candlelight—"and afterward, no one will be able to stomach looking at your face!"

Ghosts fly in and out of my cell without my say and now a letter appears from someone I never met. In the oakum room, I glance at Ivy whenever I dare. She doesn't turn her head lately; she was silent the night we all spoke of the letter and has been so since. Edwina and Rose won't stop speaking of it, but not Ivy, who fills her head with Jack. *She's with him and not here. Another one haunted by a man.* If she said she'd go, I would too. Her face on walks is often closed as if she is shutting everything out.

She won't even meet my gaze. It gets like this with all of us at times.

I sigh. Some days, the oakum draws you in. You let it. There's a secret as you work it. I wonder if the others guess.

It's this: you don't need your mind to do it, just your body. Your hands can work without you. They will untwist, straighten, unwind, flatten, roll, and fray, over and over again. While you float and watch. When you finally come out of the spell, you are altogether different. What seemed a pressing weight before now seems like nothing. Pounds of strands caked together with thick black tar, a million barbs to prick your bare flesh, have taught me this.

It's then I think of a time when I was "innocent and very different," as the letter asked. Such a time I remember, when I was my father's daughter and trusted all I met. There was Emma then, whose father owned the theater, much older than me, like a big sister. Her heart-shaped face always lit when she saw me. A playmate, loose and free as the curls spilling out of her bonnet. But on the day I returned from my mother's burial, she did not skip to see me as she usually did. Instead, her arms wrapped around me and held me in a circle. It seemed an eternity. When she let go, she had become more than a friend and sister—a mother too.

The home is named Urania. I've finally remembered

who Urania was: a Muse! One who inspires. One you call upon when there's something yearned for. She was a long-ago Grecian goddess of stars and space, places where everything is possible and nothing is known. A poem about Urania once recited suddenly floods my mind:

> She sang of night that clothed the infant world,
> In strains as solemn as its dark profound—
> How at the call of Jove the mist unfurled,
> And o'er the swelling vault—the glowing sky,
> The new-born stars hung out their lamps on high.

My mother's dress floods my mind. So far away and long gone, nothing much else remains of her. It was my mother who once chanted this verse, dressed in a twilight gown with sequins like stars on it. It's her voice I remember most. It was full of music. Sometimes it sounded like lutes and sometimes like drums. So splendid was her costume and that voice, she carried me away, up into the sky in that performance, as if she were Urania herself.

That very afternoon, after dinner, I ask for a quill and paper. Within the hour, Doyle brings them and stands over me, her neck stretched out long like a chicken's and her mouth fallen open, as if she's never seen writing before. All the girls pretend not to stare.

I wish to come, I tell the one who says he is a friend.

Hester watches with narrowed eyes.

·· ● ··

The doctor's hair is clipped at sharp angles, his skin scrubbed pink, and his nails trimmed. His white coat is spotlessly stiff. He takes his metal instruments out.

You remember the last time: in the hospital. Your body splayed on a cot, your wrists tied together. After they were done, my monthly bleeding never came anymore.

He motions me to an examining table. I must sit up in my thin gown, though I shiver.

"Any complaints about your health, E22?"

I shake my head. He sticks something into my mouth, then probes my jaw and neck with his long fingers, hunting for something. When he puts a cold metal circle to my chest, we both listen to my jumpy heart. The metal heads lower.

"Do you move your bowels regularly?"

I know to nod.

"Do you have your bleeding regularly each month?"

A quicker nod.

"Any pus? Or pain? Any unusual discharge down there?"

He's reading my records. I jump off the table. Heat rushes to my face.

But he persists. "Show me your undergarments. Pull them down so I can see if they are soiled."

His eyes scan my hips.

My bare feet walk a safe distance away. I unroll my undergarments and turn them inside out for him to see.

"If you will not let me examine your privates for disease, the examination is not complete, and I cannot recommend you for the Home. Only healthy candidates are accepted, girls clean inside and out."

We watch one another. The air thins.

"Nurse!" he shouts.

A nurse runs in and guides me to the table. "Do as the doctor says. Lie down quiet. It won't take long."

My eyes dart back and forth between them. The doctor stands in the doorway, blocking my way. I lie down while my gown is lifted and the nurse spreads my legs. Hands pin me down. Fingers dig inside me. Slime drips down my leg.

This is the place only Luther touched.

The air thickens with my screams. Then suddenly it's over and the doctor sits down to write something.

With a wave of his hand, I am dismissed.

There is a price to apply for the Home, and I have surely paid it.

·· ● ··

That night I thrash in my hammock. Toss and kick the covers off. Images swirl. The hospital walls were a sickening green, covered with decades of grease and blood.

"Did you kill it?" the nurse demanded.

"Something was sliding as I ran. I didn't know what it was."

She sneered. "Did you do something to force it out?"

"Did you wrap the cord around its neck?" accused the doctor. "For that's how it was found. And the baby blue."

I wanted to cover my ears and not hear it.

They would not tell me whether it was a boy or girl and though I begged to see it, none would bring it for the shame of being an unmarried girl. Finally I was told the babe was in the morgue awaiting autopsy. Next morning, charges were shouted out by a constable and I was taken away to face the judge at the Old Bailey, then sentenced at once to Tothill. I never saw the poor creature. Or ever named it. It was not mine. It was his.

I must have slept. In the morning I awaken in the hammock with the taste of blood in my throat.

·· ● ··

Foster, with me at her heels, descends down and down to the ground floor of the prison. Her back ramrod straight, lips pressed flat, her boots stomp ahead as if marching me down to Hell.

Sounds of the street echo upward: clomping of horses' hooves, shouts of boys, wind screeching through crevices. From their posts on each and every landing, the male guards stare down. Cold eyes knowing everything there is to know about me, eyes that have pried greedily through my chart reading the defilements.

I shouldn't be going down to him.

Hester pressed against me in line yesterday, her warning still shivering down my back: "He'll shove God down your throat like all the rest. You'll be scrubbing floors on your knees reciting bloody Hail Marys till you're thirty and near dead!"

My thin boots stall. Foster turns.

"Don't tarry, E22!"

I made a mistake.

In a second, I could fly back up the two stories quicker than a shout. But Foster closes in on me, edging her face so near mine the black whiskers above her lips poke out like stiff quills.

"Best we don't keep the gent waiting." Her words spit out in a cloud of fried eel breath.

She squeezes my elbow between her icy fingers and walks me down the landing and then along a long hallway, leading me to a room with its door swung wide open.

"Sir? E22 is here."

A smallish gentleman sits at a table, papers before him. Immediately his eyes fix on me as if eyeing oysters in a stall. The iron maiden knuckles my back. I inch forward and sit down where he points, in a chair facing him. Suddenly my breath catches in my throat. I try to breathe from deep in my belly as Pa taught me to do for stage fright but it tugs at my throat instead.

"Welcome, Miss Wood. I am Mr. Dickens. I'm here to interview you for admission to Urania, the Home a private benefactor, Miss Coutts, has established for girls who have...gone astray. Those who might welcome a second chance. Such help we offer certain girls. I was told that you yourself wrote the letter asking to meet with me. Is that correct?"

I nod, breath held. No one has said my last name since the day I left court to come directly here.

The man is crisp and finely dressed. A blur of something soft underneath his brown jacket. A vest as smooth as rabbit, the color of sapphire. Velvet!

"What was your schooling?"

He opens a thick black leather book and dips a quill in blue ink.

"Mostly my pa, sir, who taught me to read aloud and memorize. And then to write when he wasn't so...I didn't stay long at the ragged school they sent us to for free."

"Which one were you sent to in your neighborhood?"

"Old Penny Square, sir."

An image rises up between the two of us: a crowd of shouting boys, hands down my dress or in my pockets whenever the schoolmaster turned his back. Mr. Dickens grows still at my words. I swear he is seeing my very own thoughts.

"Then you are from Devil's Acre, the Irish rookery, in the parish of Westminster." He tilts his head as I nod.

The rookery. Hundreds crammed inside tiny crumbling houses. Families of ten stuffed inside a single room. Throngs pouring out into the streets in summer's heat. Never quiet, except in the middle of the night, when Luther roamed.

"Does your family live there now? It's so close by, you must have many visitors at Tothill."

My breath catches in my throat. "He…my…pa is dead, sir."

"I am sorry to hear it. And your mother?"

"They said too late you cannot drink of the Thames. Cholera swarmed in the water. Many died that year. My mother was one."

"How old were you then? This must have been… forty-nine?"

"Yes, sir. I was nearly nine. Afterward, I only had Pa two more years. He never was the same."

Sometimes Pa would stop in the middle of listening to a speech I had memorized and stare into the distance until I called him back into the room.

He lost his muse, his Urania, my mother. I know that now; I didn't then.

"Is there no one else in the rookery to welcome you home?"

Not my aunt on Great St. Anne's Lane. I can never go back there. My first home was the theater on Old Pye Street where I was born. Behind its stage lived Emma and her father. In a narrow hallway upstairs, Pa and I stayed until he died and they took me away.

Soon as my eyes opened each morning, Pa still snoring in a drunken daze, I ran down to Emma. I was by that girl's side every hour back then. Always she shared breakfast and lessons in reading and writing when Pa could not. Between us, we sneaked the latest installment of stories sold in the street, reading them to one another and collapsing in giggles.

She wouldn't want to know the kind of girl I have become.

I stare at Mr. Dickens without answering. The man watches everything and absorbs it as if the world is kindling and he a bonfire. Even Foster's bone of a face peering in by the door where she stands guard, head turned, listening, he sees.

Suddenly, the gentleman leaps up from the desk. In three quick steps, he bounds to Foster, grabs her sleeve, and whispers in her ear. Foster disappears from the door. I am now alone and face-to-face with this man. He nods for me to continue.

Only my thoughts grow bold: *One is alive who I wish*

dead. Another lives, the only one who cared—Emma. Most certainly dead I would be had I not been sent to Tothill. "Only one...perhaps. The others—"

"Where are they now?"

Emma's letter is hidden between the bricks of my cell wall since Christmas, growing dark and wet with the damp.

"Nowhere to be found, sir."

The fierce scratching of his quill surprises me. The man's hand flies across the paper as if pursued. *What he is saying about me in that black book, I dread to guess. That I am not suitable, I already know. Whatever made him think to come to a prison to find a good girl?*

"Now I must ask you about your crimes. I am not here to condemn but to understand. What you say will not be reported to any prison authority, I assure you."

Each word is a road. To conceal. To talk around. Or to tell. All the air suddenly leaves me so that I feel faint. I lean far back from him, toward the hard wall.

"Can you tell me why you were taken here?"

"I was found in the street, sir. And then...taken to hospital. After...the way I was found...they said I had committed a crime against society."

"What was this crime?"

Mr. Dickens stops writing and lifts his eyes to mine.

"They branded me a fallen girl. They had the evidence."

"Which was?"

"There on the street, sir…a baby spilled out of me. Too fast. Too early. Didn't know it was coming. I must have fainted. When I woke, I was in hospital. Constables stood by the door ready to take me away once the bleeding slowed."

Silence. Long minutes pass. Finally he reaches for a single paper upon the desk bearing an official stamp.

"According to your record," he says while I grab the chair bottom hard, "the charges against you were these: infanticide. Prostitution. Robbery. Your aunt and uncle both disowned you for being with child."

"Please sir, I am innocent of all those charges. But no one believed me."

Mr. Dickens raises his eyebrows. "Witnesses had seen you through the windows of Silver Feathers, a brothel. A man's wallet was missing. A baby died. And you refused to name the baby's father."

"What was done was done, sir. A man damned me. Many times I've wished him dead."

"His name?"

I sit still as a rock. I can harden my whole body that way.

The quill scratches at breakneck speed, then stops. The gentleman stares at me for what seems like hours.

Finally Mr. Dickens sighs. "Do you have any questions of me?"

Questions boil up inside me like live eels in a pot. All

slithering in circles and biting their own tails to get out. But I shake my head.

He tells me more of Urania, Home for lost girls. Rules are enforced there: punctuality, cleanliness, household chores such as cooking, cleaning and knitting, education, and prayer. The first few months, a girl is on probation. When the term is over, arrangement is made to transport her to a position in the colonies as a maid or possibly a governess. For it is impossible to return to London society once so fallen.

But I lose most of it, for when he says there will be a library of many books and a garden too and that the Home sits in the countryside outside London, I almost stand to run right there. Pictures fill my mind: green fields; a soft bed; far away and safe from Luther. That man cast his shadow over the whole rookery. I shall always feel his chill lurking around every corner, a readiness to pounce, should I return there.

My hands squeeze into a solid block beneath the desk but I do not budge lest Mr. Dickens see how eager I am. If I could escape from here to there, I could be Orpha again. Even if I had to scrub all the floors.

"I will think on it, sir," I promise him as I curtsy on my way out.

Mr. Dickens, you have dangled a sugarplum in my face. Shall I take your bait?

Another girl recommended by Governor Tracey. Her Red Star speaks for itself. Most inmates enter this prison multiple times, but not her. Not yet. At sixteen, she's the most literate inmate I've encountered.

The girl is pale and so still she could have been Marble. Indeed she hardly breathes, her chest slight and birdlike. Her family has deserted her. But she shares no plans and does not think to ask questions about what we offer.

She winces when asked about her crimes, suggesting Contrition and great pain. Malnourished, Underweight, Secretive—although they all are to have survived the streets.

Most impressive is her Handwriting. It's written in a tidy hand with no misspellings. Most girls I interview can neither read or write. So much time is taken teaching them at the Home.

There is more to her and I wish to know it.

CD

· ● · ·

Out on the Devil's Walk today, by the shelter of the wall, the Head Matron spits out orders as if training horses, heading us into the cutting wind.

"Left!" "About face! "To the right!" Then, "Stop! To the left!"

The other matrons quicken to follow us. Doyle huffs and puffs as she marches beside us, expecting the lot of us to run at a quick pace. We do. She turns toward the Head Matron with a wide grin as if to proudly show off her charges doing her bidding. Harred casts a sour look our way.

Edwina shuffles. Her legs can't quite keep her straight up. Between us, the rope slackens and I yank it hard to help her stand. She sniffs loudly and spits, cap tumbling to the ground. Her scalp is patchy and nearly bald. In the middle of the night, I awoke to matrons shushing someone's cries. Could they have been hers?

At the turn, Hester slices a dark look my way. She won't dare call out from the head of the rope but I guess the words she'd like to yell: "Don't you go!"

"Did you meet the letter writer?" Ivy's words fly in a wind toss of low notes.

Two tugs on the rope reach her hands with a yes.

On the next round, my back to the matrons, I dare throw my words.

"Won't you see him too?"

Ivy shakes her head.

"You'll be educated, Ivy! You won't have to commit crimes!"

Ivy's free hand slides over her heart: *Jack!* I say no more. If her mind weren't so set on that man, we could be together in the Home. Instead of sneaking words on the rope-walk and shouts in the dark, risks that could condemn us both to the dark cell, we could tell one another everything there. Ivy wouldn't ever return to Tothill then. She'd be with me.

·· THREE ··

Along E corridor is the unlucky cell: E25. Matrons must think it so too, for it remains empty though new prisoners arrive weekly. It is shunned like the crossroads by Hobart Place where London's suicides are buried but not resting at all.

"The suicide" was how we spoke of the last girl in that cell, who had tried to take her own life twice before she was sent here. No older than fourteen, murky-faced as the Thames, she was drawn into herself. In the yard, we yanked her along with us on the rope-walk, for she was a dead weight.

She was sent to the darks for refusing to come out of her cell to chapel. "God never saved me from him!" she shouted. No threats from the matrons could stop the howling. In the end, she was dragged to Bedlam, a hospital that houses the insane. She never returned from there. If you enter madness, there is no way out.

One thing can change your life forever. Never in the way anyone would wish. Now a gentleman offers to change everything. Mr. Dickens is very polished, the kind of man, rich and important, one might see attending the

Theater Royal instead of the run-down theater where we performed. Or perhaps the man is only pretending to be so. Most of us pretend to be other than we are. Ivy surely did. My own father burrowed like a worm inside his characters, propped all evening long on a stool at the Black Horse, reciting drunken lines to an audience that was not there.

Best to stop thinking. Keep busy. Time seems to stand still but it is actually moving tho' all of us feel it stalled. Think only on what's left of the sentence. I count my time ahead in days now. Ivy looks backward at what was lost.

I bend down to the oakum. Having a task divides time so I don't bear its crushing weight all at once. Time can melt into little bits that way. If I can pluck this pile of oakum, I tell myself, then I can go on.

·· ● ··

"You two!" Foster shouts in the lineup, pointing to the slop buckets.

It's mostly the bigger girls who carry the buckets down. Ivy and I lift a bucket in each hand as Foster trails us down the hallway. Backs pulled rigid. Lead-footed steps so the pails don't tilt. Inside, in the frothy yellow urine, feces slide back and forth. As we head down the steps, Ivy presses her lips tight. I don't hear her until we are halfway down the stairs. Giggles!

On the bottom floor, we head farther down, onto the steps leading to the basement, along a corridor and then to a doorway emitting a fetid stink.

"In there!" Foster halts. "No spilling!"

The matron doesn't enter with us. Instead, she paces the hall outside.

Together, we edge across the cold room, where dampness seeps out of the walls as if the Thames itself surrounded us. Ahead is a huge open pipe that leads underground. It is smeared with feces and monthlies blood and ancient urine. I can hardly breathe for the odor.

"What luck!" Ivy laughs. "To be picked together. We can talk here! They don't know we're pals. Been watching you all this time and guessed you didn't do any of it, did you? None of those crimes?"

I shake my head.

"You're an innocent, as I once was as a child. Someone sure hammered the nails into you at that Old Bailey. When we get out of here, we've both got to steer clear of it."

We lift our buckets and begin the slow pour but immediately lean back. Urine sloshes upward, barely missing our cheeks.

I turn my head. "But you're going back to Jack. Whatever for?"

Ivy leans back, eyes on the door, as she pours. "I was nine years old when he found me. My grandma had died, the only one I had left. I was living on the streets. Chased by boys who stole my only shoes and beat me whenever they could. Jack pulled me away from them. Said he'd take care of me. I was starving. So I went with him. Into a gang of counterfeiters."

"But why did you stay?" I gasp.

"He fed me. Taught me his trade. Not once did he push me to be his girl. I decided that later on myself. He was my first. And only."

Boot stomps at the door.

"Hurry it up in there!" booms Foster, a handkerchief over her nose and mouth, before stepping back from the ammonia smell and disappearing.

"He got you in here!" I whisper right in her ear.

Ivy shakes her head. "I knew the risk. But I wasn't afraid. Besides, we needed to eat. He's my only family. I wouldn't have survived without him. He taught me how to listen and look dumb to know all there is to know. Like how I heard of you from the matrons' gossiping, your name and your crime. Didn't believe them one bit."

All the buckets are empty now. We step toward the door.

"Am I your family too?" I cry.

"You are like a sister to me. You saw into my soul as I saw into yours."

Out in the hallway, just before Foster turns our way, Ivy lines up behind me, whispering into the bones of my back. "I'll make him go clean. You'll see. We'll be together, all three of us. You'll come live with—"

But we have entered silence once again. The only sounds are the metal pails swinging back and forth, back and forth, and the drumbeat of Foster's heels right behind us.

·· ● ··

They refuse to let us into the airing yards today. Gray skies day after day and now snow. It swirls through the yard in gusts and shakes the windowpanes. Carts from the prison library rattle past in the oakum room as matrons hand out books to those who want them. Most refuse. Not Ivy or me. Edwina studies the pictures only. Ivy's fingers trace the lines and stop. Her lips silently try to form syllables. If only I could whisper the difficult words to her. But Doyle stands watching. I grab *Robinson Crusoe*, about a castaway on an island, a man who teaches himself how to survive alone. I need to find out how he does it. But there is never enough time to escape with him. Already the light is low and so dusky, the book's print fades away. Drafts pry beneath the layers of my cloak. Hours to go before supper.

I study the Red Star girls around me, sisters all. Hester sneers at our armbands. She's never had one. Matrons hint that the star earns us something upon discharge. I hope that means coins.

Six new girls arrive today, all crown debtors, plenty of them now that it is winter. Their sentence is under two weeks, their arms bannerless, their crimes minor. None could pay the small fine the court slammed them with, so they work the oakum to pay off their debt. Most are on the verge of laughing, glad to be fed and to wear shoes for a time. The only thing they miss is the drink.

One has a blackened eye with purple streaking her face down to the chin. Her prison gown slants off her shoulder. Another has a swollen nose. Their work is sloppy and often handed back. Some yank with their front teeth to chew the tar away. All keep watch for the supper pots. They hold fire inside. Not like us in F corridor: pale indoor girls whose eyes have lost any light they once held.

One of the debtors has a cunning sneer and a bloodlike unnatural color to her hair. She drills her gaze at Hester, who glares right back. This girl will be free soon. I force my bonnet down. But the image holds: her flushed face, tipped-up chin, that knowing smirk.

I must leave the room. It is unbearable. So I will myself away.

Somewhere an hourglass slowly shifts. I roam. Daring to drift back to Emma. Quickstepping up and down the stairs, playing hide-and-seek, belly-laughing, jumping across hidden passageways and gangplanks, feet flying in the air, my eyes landing on hers as she grabbed my hands back to safety over the abyss. What a great thump we made!

Let her remember me that way. May she never be certain that I am at Tothill. May she never be told.

Then, in an instant, the hourglass slams upside down and I cannot stop its sands from dropping. The other one sneaks in: Luther. The one who shows up when I least expect him to, when I am low and on my knees. He can slip through the barred windows like sewer slime. Sometimes my eyes catch the glint of his blade.

Matrons commend the ferocity with which I pick oakum.

"This one's a real baby killer!" Doyle roars, watching my fingers viciously pluck the rope as if ripping feathers from dead chickens.

No one sees how the tar rips my palms, making them bleed, darkening the rope. When they cart the oakum off to repair the boats on the Thames, that blood will stain those filthy brown waters red.

You! It's the skin you cannot shed. Ever!

•• • ••

Almost dark. Nearby, Ivy and Rose slip into their cells like ghosts. Suddenly a wave of stink floats past, nearly choking me. Now I can name that putrid smell: flesh rotting in an open grave. One never forgets a stench like that.

Foster slams the cell door shut behind my back. Alone, I wonder if that stench is me. Perhaps I am hemorrhaging again as I did for weeks when I first came here, after the childbirth. Not since then has there been any monthly. Quickly I lift my skirts and swipe a finger against the coarse prison underwear. It's dry.

I think back to that time at Aunt Agatha's house on Great St. Anne's Lane where I lived for over a year after the workhouse. Something had happened to my body. Telltale signs I never guessed: swollen breasts, how cooking grease turned my stomach and that pressure, pulsing deep down. I had no say in its existence inside me.

When I look up, the walls lean inward. *There is nowhere to go. Not now. Not ever. Even in a refuge, I will be found out.*

I fling my fists at the hard stone, which does not budge, then slam my stomach flat into the wall. But it still does not move. Just like Luther. It's him I want to push until I am no more and all that ever happened to me never did. *Him!* If I could sneak up behind him, catch him unaware, stab his own Valentin deep into him before

I wrestle the blade out of his guts and slice open my own belly for not knowing what a man could do to a girl.

His lying testimony in court. "The girl's trash. Everyone knew she was a ladybird at that Silver Feathers. More than once, she tried to stab me!"

Footsteps pound closer. I press my back against the cold wall, sipping my breath as the eyelet clicks open.

·· FOUR ··

Hard matron's boots clunk to my cell door and stop.
Just her boot slam tells me who it is. Foster stomps over
the stone floor as if she'd like to flatten us all.

"Gent's waiting downstairs. Move!"

Two visits in two weeks. The rule is broken. I bow
my head in case the matron catches the questions in my
eyes, the sweet delight.

Mr. Dickens calls me back.

The gentleman is not sitting quietly this time but
pacing the length of the room, hands behind his back.
He does not stop either while we stand and wait in the
doorway. Not until Foster clears her throat thrice does
he turn our way, looking at us sharply as if in a dream or
perhaps a nightmare. He immediately motions me to my
chair and nods for the matron to leave us. Foster retreats
out of earshot down the long hallway, her eyes scraping
my face like a knife's edge.

Mr. Dickens sits at last, lifts his quill, and writes in a
thick notebook this time, not in the dreadful black prison
log. He takes no notice of me. From upside down, facing the desk, his jottings don't seem like words at all but

odd slashes and squiggles. His quill scratches the page as crisp as claws cutting through paper.

Then, like a fit, it's over. He slips the notebook into a traveling bag. "Miss Wood, I'd like to determine how well you read. Can you read aloud to me from this?"

He slides a book across the table, careful to keep his fingertips only on the side nearest him. "Flip it open. Any page will do."

"*Sketches by Boz*!" A little shout pops out of me. "A *whole* book?"

"You know it?"

"Yes, sir! In here is everyday London and Seven Dials too. Pa used to say that though the poor are the dregs of society, Boz loves us. 'London will take notice!' he swore. But it didn't come as a book at all."

"Then you read it in monthly installments?"

"Whenever we could. From hand to hand, we passed it around and shared its one-shilling price. Wrapped in green paper, it arrived like gold treasure. When Pa read it aloud, he taught me the trick of holding the words inside to remember them. I recited it back to him word for word."

The book's binding spreads wide open before me to a painting of "The Gin-Shop" in the rookery, at the bottom of Tottenham Road. I nearly stop breathing. No pictures were inside the installments. All I can do is stare at the barrels, their names boasting: "*The real*

Knock-me-Down!" "The Cream of the Valley!" "The Out and Out!" This was the tavern and these the names, the promises of power. Yanking Pa out with his pockets empty every single night after my mother died, steering him back to our hallway room. Luther slipping in like a shadow, leaving taller, lit, sneering.

"Miss Wood?" The soft voice interrupts.

If only my hands had parted another page. If only I didn't have to remember it all over again, what happened to Pa. For a time, he was true. That's how I wish to remember him. Not in the gin shop. Not his spending every penny on drink and borrowing more. Not what came afterward.

I begin to read aloud through gritted teeth how in the slums, amid dirt and poverty, gin shops shine their brightest gaslights, while at home, most can barely afford candlelight. But, just around the block, Boz writes:

Wretched houses with broken windows patched with rags and paper: every room let out to a different family, and in many instances to two or even three... barbers and red-herring vendors in the front parlors, cobblers in the back; a bird-fancier on the first floor, three families on the second, starvation in the attics... and a charwoman and five hungry children in the back one—filth everywhere.

My voice wavers.

"Tell it from inside," I hear Pa coax his company of actors. "Let your pain bleed into Hamlet's soliloquy. Become Hamlet and leave your own self behind."

I slip inside the words like second skin, pronouncing the characters' accents properly. Think ahead as Pa trained me, hearing his voice speak the lines. Sounds lift off the page: the clink of glasses being raised in toasts, drunks weeping, shouts and brawls spilling out into the streets. My mouth feels dry, parched like the toothless old men who crept in, pointing to a barrel as if it were an elixir to turn them young again.

Pa has come into the room! He could rant up there on the stage so no one in the whole rude crowd called out or even coughed.

At the chapter's end, I look up. The sun is gone from the window. Mr. Dickens is sitting quite still, a hand clasped over his beard and his jaw parted.

"You read as if speaking to an audience, Miss Wood. You don't laugh at the sarcasm, yet it's there in your voice. How difficult it must have been to be sent here." He sweeps his arm around the room. "In this silence and killing isolation round the clock. How do you bear it?"

If I say too much, I will damn myself. But if I don't tell him enough, he will lose interest.

"When my hands are busy with oakum, I don't mind as much."

"I hope you shall have better work when you are released, Miss Wood. Do you have any home to go to?"

I shake my head.

"How do you get along with the other inmates?"

"I'm afraid of them, sir. So I keep quiet. And think on my sins."

"Have you any friends from the rookery?"

I shrug.

"Surely someone could visit you here? Yet the log shows no one came. Have you told any of your friends that you are here?"

I shake my head. *No one must know. Not Emma ever.*

His head tilts slightly. "Friends and family could help you survive this place. In hope of seeing them once again. Are you certain no one in the rookery could help you?"

He doesn't know about the friendship of Ivy or the others—inmates whose names and crimes I know. Voices in the dark telling me: *There are other girls like you who barely sinned, sisters all. We are among the fallen.*

"At times, I am not alone, sir, though this place is most harsh."

After a long pause, he speaks about the dead-end alleys that trap young girls: how once fallen, they must survive penniless in the streets without education, skills, or husbands, drifting into prostitution, then into prisons and asylums. My whole body feels naked.

Surely he means Hester and girls like her. Not Ivy or Rose or Edwina. We got the letters, after all. But Ivy will return to her smasher because she doesn't know any other way. And they say when Rose lost her factory job, she begged in the streets. That's what put her here in the first place—a second offense for begging, caught taking money from a man in the street, so they supposed the worst. Edwina's a mystery, as old as Hester but resembling a sickly child. Whatever she did, I can't guess.

Every time I think of a future, a wall slams down. *There's nowhere to go!*

Mr. Dickens writes in the black log now. His quill circles slowly and halts before he huddles over in his chair to write once more. He is making judgment upon me for answers I refuse to give him.

"Sir." I lean forward. "I have a question."

Mr. Dickens does not raise his head from the log.

"Whatever happened to Boz, sir? Pa said his name was once spoken on every street corner. Does he still write?"

His quill immediately stops. "He is very much alive and writing still. You shall likely read his work again someday."

The gentleman actually smiles, his cheeks pinking. "It will soon be spring, Miss Wood, and you will be released from Tothill. Daffodils will be blooming by then. You must make plans."

"*I wandered lonely as a cloud—*" I quote, just as Pa taught me.

"*—that floats on high o'er vales and hills,*" he finishes the line.

"*When all at once, I saw a crowd / A host of golden daffodils…*"

As I recite the rest of Wordsworth's poem, the quill drops from Mr. Dickens's hand. The gentleman twists his head to one side and his eyes do not leave mine.

INTERVIEW NUMBER 2 WITH ORPHA WOOD

The girl is careful with her words, measuring each and every one on a scale. She folds into herself before answering my questions, plotting.

Like most prisoners, she has become invisible and doesn't share much of herself. Who can blame her? Or did it happen long before Tothill? Give me a girl with fire. She will burn to get what she wants.

Yet to watch Orpha read and recite is to see another being emerge: an Actress who flows, someone who was loved once.

There's Fire there somewhere. Can a girl like Orpha come alive again if given a second chance? Or is it already too late?

CD

·· FIVE ··

Rose disappears. The odor in the corridor vanishes with her. Ivy's eyes greet me each morning with darkness deeper than the day before. Not one signal does she send in the silent oakum room. Even when I flip my hand in front of her, the sign to ask how she is doing, she doesn't respond. The others won't look my way either. Only the Red Star girls grant me a nod. Hester glares, her mouth in a flat line.

Then down to work in the oakum factory. New faces appear. No one notices the crown debtors leaving. They just slip out one day. New faces immediately replace them as if there are lineups in the street waiting to fill Tothill.

All that morning, a child's howl fills the factory. It's a sound that sinks my heart down to my stomach. A11, a small girl, just arrived, chants over and over, "Lemme go home, ma'am!" Tiny, with an upturned nose and dusting of freckles, she looks about eight. Snot crusts her lips. Such a girl has likely never spent an hour away from her family. Her band is yellow: she'll stay three months. Her life is changed forever. She knows it too.

On the way back to our cells after dinner, two matrons escort a new inmate into E25, the suicide's cell.

She grabs hold of her shaved head and shrieks as if on fire. Her eyes dart wildly but do not land on us. I'd guess her age as thirteen. Short and knock-kneed, she cringes as the matrons shove her into the cell. She is still begging them to let her free when they bolt the door in her face.

All evening we wait on it. In full dark, it begins. Thumps. A body thrown at a door. More thumps. Fists pound against stone walls and then the screaming begins. It's a smash-up.

It sets off the rest of us like wild animals sniffing prey. One after another, inmates kick their cell doors and bang with bare fists, setting the metal eyelets chattering like teeth. Hester's in the lead, no doubt, like a great she-wolf calling her pack in for the kill.

Matrons' boots beat down the hallways, slamming their sticks along walls and against cell doors, threatening to smack us. All inmates cease their clanging at once. Like rats, we scurry to the eyelets to listen.

A door creaks open. "What's this racket!" Foster demands. "What have you done to your uniform? And your hammock?"

"Don't leave me here all alone!" E25's voice rises shrill and high. "I never meant to go on the lift and steal. I was starving!"

"You'll stay here or else there's another place to send you!" Doyle shouts. "To the darks! If you don't hush!"

The girl pleads. High-pitched yells. Then sharp slaps. Her screams grow louder. No one comes to help. I step away and meet the solid wall at my back. My body drops to the floor, arms wrapped around my belly like ropes, inert as a bundle of oakum.

Matrons' boots march to each cell and stop. There is a matron at my very own cell door, slipping the eyelet open to peek at me crouched on the floor, where I have shrunk down, hands covering my head. Her breath sharpens as she clicks the eyelet shut. All night long, boots kick up and down the hall. Just when I think them gone for the night, they bang back.

Then the yellow fog that plagues this city, bubbling and brewing from factories and furnaces and black rivers, rolls into my cell, stinking of coal and tar and excrement. Thick and clammy like his body. The smell of stagnant sewer water seeps in. A terrible face forms within the fog cloud, with leering lips and long fingers reaching out.

He's come.

My body flattens and I cover my ears. I don't know where the gasps are coming from, louder and shriller by the moment. The silvery Valentin shines, reflecting in his bottomless black eyes.

I try to shove my fists through his slippery face. But I can't get at him. Just when my fingers close around Luther's muddy throat, he slips away. There's a yank at my foot and he's dragging me in circles. Something stiff is jammed against my leg, and I push it away, reeling in his grasp, upon the cold battling floor.

His thick, wide hands pin me down. Bare hands that smashed rats' heads, smearing their bloody brains against a ditch many a time, he told me so himself. And the weight of him, a hundred sacks of grain dropped on top of me so not a breath escapes my lungs. All my organs pulse, my stomach pumping up toward the tight cord of my mouth.

And then his grimy fists slam down over my lips when they open wide to scream "Pa!" Who never came. Ever.

No one hears me. I pound. No one comes. My palms are sore and swollen from blaming the stone floor.

·· • ··

It is very dark in the cell. I drift above, looking down at a girl, her cap askew, collar soaked with tears. She's wearing a dull gray prison uniform. Surely she's in costume, ready to perform the next scene.

A girl who has lost all sense, matrons will write in their night journal.

I lift myself from the floor and walk to the wash-basin to wash my face in the dark, find my bonnet and slip it on, then crawl into my hammock and force myself to shut my eyes. Try to rock myself to calmness and open a way for Pa. He's a blanket to wrap myself with. I try not to think of those last years. How when Ma slipped away, he let go of me too.

·· ● ··

In the morning, I awaken to gunfire and dress quickly, then stand at attention, waiting for inspection. Foster orders me onto the threshold of the cell, her sneer almost a smile. She strips my uniform of the Red Star and shoves it into her pocket with the other armbands. Then she snatches *Robinson Crusoe* out of my hands, but I tug it back until she yells for another matron. I let go then.

"You'll never set eyes on this book again!" she shouts.

·· ● ··

There is no chapel today. Breakfast is delivered through the eyelet into my cell: half a ration of toke and a jug of cold water. Before the eyelet shuts, I peek out quickly. No comings and goings of the other girls. Only the matron's boots bang back and forth. So all of us are being punished then. Ivy will be standing as I am, looking out toward the hallway and going nowhere. Pray she keeps quiet. Pray she doesn't call out. She hates confinement more than I do. "The longer the time, the heavier it weighs on you," she once told me. "As if there is no future, only this Hell forever." *Let her bear it.*

By supper, the chamber pot attracts flies that circle and buzz. Piss turns the air acid. Out of the corner of my eye, a flash of something scurries in the far corner: rat's tail or Luther. The walls lean in.

The cell space shrinks just as it did when I first came here. That's when I learned to pace: to prove to myself that the cell did not change. If I could measure it, if it was still six steps across and eight steps long, it calmed me. If I could walk it, my body seemed solid.

I pace in circles, then suddenly stop, remembering my fit. Was it when I first came here, like the new girl, or was it just last night? It must have been last night too. No wonder I am punished. Of course there will be a report and all our names in E corridor will be listed. What will Mr. Dickens say? *Her record is blemished; she is capable of losing control; no longer is she acceptable for the Home.*

"Better send her to Bedlam instead!" the matrons will hiss.

·· • ··

On the second morning, I pry loose the letter from between the bricks where it's been hidden these two months.

Dearest Orpha,

I've searched for you all through the rookery. Pa finally found your aunt on Great St. Anne's Lane. She was spitting mad to hear of you. Said you'd run off with all their money. Nasty woman!

But now word has spread over Devil's Acre. Is it true? Are you really at Tothill? I write this in hopes of finding you there, my heart broken if you are. Tell me the truth and I will come.

Your friend,
Emma

How to untangle the many mazes of lies for her? They are labyrinths. I tuck the letter deeper into the brick.

·· ● ··

On the third morning, they let us out. Lined up in the hallway, I blink at the high, open space. Sunlight brightens the walls and fresh, cool air rises up from the bottom floor like spring. All the girls are pale with flyaway hair and caps askew as if they had slept in a rats' nest. Ivy stumbles out of her cell unsteady on her feet, cheeks drawn and shoulders hunched. Her flat lips puff out a silent *O* like a wail. Her palms bang together: *I'd like to smash them!* Hester sports a sly smile, like a cat who has cornered a mouse.

E25 joins us at chapel, escorted by two matrons, one at each elbow. Both her arms are locked behind in cuffs, and leather belts bind her hands to her waist. One of her eyes is blackened and her face purpled with bruises.

In the midst of the girls at chapel, I open my mouth

wide. Listen! A wild animal, with fangs and claws and wings, howls how it fell asleep in a forest and awakened in a cage. It is not me.

Ivy raps on the wooden wall between us.

"Stop that! They'll hear you!"

"I can't do this any longer."

"Neither can I. But you mustn't let them see you like this."

I keep on wailing.

"I said stop! You have less than a month left. They can add more time, you know."

I shut my mouth after that.

That afternoon, Rose joins us in lineup to go outside. She was not punished, luckily, for she was in the infirmary and not with us. One side of her face is bandaged. Something bulges underneath, pushing the bindings out. Her eyes are puffy and red. That rotting odor follows behind her like a presence. I catch her wincing as she circles around in the rope-walk, heading into the stinging spring wind, bracing her left cheek tight to her shoulder.

·· ● ··

Girls from E wing are handed motley piles of rope. Stiffened with clumps of pine tar like an old man's arthritic limbs, only heavy tugging can tame it.

From her high seat, Harred gloats, fixing me like a

butterfly on a pin, writing notes in her black prison log. Sometimes she whispers to the other matrons, chin held high, tracking me with her stare. Or is it since Mr. Dickens's visits that they've eyed me sideways? *A soiled girl*— their thoughts dart across the factory to poke me. *Used property. A fine gentleman like him wasting his precious time on that one!*

My hands punch through the oakum. The others knew to be quiet when they heard the matrons come. But Luther did not penetrate their cells with fists of iron and the sharp point of his Valentin.

From across the way, A11 weeps silently, her chest caved in. In these three days, she's thinned. Likely she hasn't eaten since being brought here.

"Passed a bad halfpenny of her mum's to buy bread and got caught red-handed." Foster elbows Doyle, pointing to the girl. "They're all trash."

"Give her one more day." Doyle's loud laughter sets her breasts bouncing. "She'll come around and eat. They all do."

It's good that Doyle is not near my boot. Tothill's matrons live here under their own lock and key. Not mothers, not wives, but spinsters. Tothill changes them first into shadow, then into stone. The one difference between us is that we will leave here. They must hate us for that.

Lint floats everywhere. I force my fingers to pick. To untwist rope into strands one by one. Wrap filaments around my forearm and grate them back and forth against my own flesh. At my feet, oakum climbs into a mountain.

My eyes land on Rose and I wish they had not. Her new binding is blood-soaked and smeared with yellow pus. The whole side of her left jaw swells, twisting her head sideways. These last two Sundays, her singing has not filled the hallway, though I often hear her humming. That afternoon, my hands worm through oakum like blind eyes seeking a way out of the dark.

But the darkness is everywhere.

When they bolt me in that evening, I lean my head against the cold cell door. It's been weeks since I heard from the gentleman. Did I imagine those conversations with Mr. Dickens? The matrons must have reported my sins to him. Better the door is locked right now, for I tremble what I would do to them, their throats flattening beneath my fists.

·· ● ··

Early next morning, it takes me by surprise. Foster points to the buckets. Once again, Ivy and I tiptoe down to the basement carrying them, arms stiffened, legs trembling. I don't dare look at her. If I see that grin of hers, I'll be damned by my own giggles.

But once inside that fetid room, I gulp. Just the two of us alone. So many words saved up to say to her. Now they jam in my throat, making it pulse.

"If he doesn't pick me, I've got nowhere to go!" I cry out. "I can't go back to the rookery, Ivy!"

"Hush!" Ivy swivels toward the door, eyes popping. "I already told you. You're coming with me and Jack."

It falls out in a whisper. "But you don't know everything about me. If only I could tell you."

"You mean . . . the baby?"

I nod.

"Something terrible happened to you. You don't need to say it."

"But I . . . I want to—"

The hard voice yells down the hallway.

"What! You put those two together? Thick as thieves, they are. No telling what they're up to."

Boot slams. Head Matron Harred stands in the doorway.

"Don't let the two of them work together again!" She points to us, Foster paling at her side. "Plenty you don't know about E21."

·· ● ··

In the hallway before we enter our cells that evening, we find out what there is to know. Ivy is handed an official letter with a broken seal. Foster reads it aloud. The news echoes throughout the corridor like a newspaper head-line shouted from the *Times:*

"Jack arrested. Pocketful of forged banknotes written in his own handwriting. Transportation to Tasmania."

Ivy sways, then almost falls. "Jack!" she screams, run-ning down the hallway as if he is standing there, so the matrons must chase after her. She's raving as they shove her into her cell backward with their hands pressed flat over her face.

My feet run. By the time I'm at her cell, she's already gone, swallowed in stone, her door slammed shut. They won't let me speak to her through the eyelet, although I scream her name and beg and pound. Foster kicks my shins, shoving me back into my own cell as they did her.

Three stone feet between us. Did she hear me call for her?

·· ● ··

It's deep in the afternoon and something has happened to time. It is standing still. No exercise today. It poured. Dry fingers grate against oakum. From the crown debt side, the redhead slices her glare right through me. Sweat breaks out on my neck. I force myself to look down at my hands. Then I look up at her again.

Her lips twist, mocking. She will be out the door at month's end when they let the new ones in.

My feet push me up.

"Back to your stool, F22!" Doyle hisses in my ear.

Suddenly there is a whir behind me. Hester flies through the air past me. She claws and smacks the red-headed girl on her face.

"Tart!" Hester screeches. "Stop staring at me like that!"

The matrons descend like hawks upon the two furies and yank both down the aisle, coatless, out to the yard.

"We'll be seeing more of this one, mark my word," snickers Doyle as she drags the redhead out.

Within fifteen minutes, the cranks begin, after the howling stops.

·· ● ··

A letter waits upon the floor of my cell when we return from Sunday chapel. It can't be good news. It never is in here.

Feed it to Luther. He loves soiled things. It's his job. He's a tosher, as was his father before him. One who descends into London's dark underworld of sewers, where he fishes out finery from the muck: rings and coins, pocket watches that slipped out of pockets and silver spoons. Greedily he grabbed them, though he stepped through a maze of rats and reeking sewer gas to get to them. I don't remember him ever bathing. All I remember are his unforgiving hands.

My boot grinds the letter into the stone. Best to

tramp it down. Around and around, I circle the cell. Beneath my boot, the letter grows filthier.

When next I look up, the light is almost gone.

From far away, loudening by the moment, a trumpeting shout is heading closer. I look up to the window, waiting to see that slice of things. A wondrous flock of wild swans crosses the thin slant of window, squawking their return home to the far-off Baltic Sea after wintering here. Their honking lingers in my bare cell long after they disappear.

They say swans carry the souls of the dead to Heaven, coming and going from the otherworld. They will carry me out of here too. When they migrate north like this, it is almost spring. My time is nearly up! They cannot keep me here. No matter what I did or did not do.

Suddenly I am on my knees crawling toward the crumpled letter. I rip it open like oakum.

Dear Miss Wood,

Pressing business and family matters have called me elsewhere. And Deadlines. However, I have been in touch with the prison and have had their reports keeping me apprised of the condition of the inmates who have applied to the Home.

The Riot in E corridor has affected me with great sadness. The matrons wrote in harsh tones about the breakdown you had in your cell and your involvement in the uprising. But I have read between their lines.

How could you not be affected by another's fear? You were driven into an old habit of Despair the night the new girl arrived. That was an Unfortunate but very normal reaction as evidenced by the behavior of all your fellow inmates. Further, the night notes clearly state that though you were "curled tight as a ball of Coif on the floor at midnight, wailing, with sheets spilled everywhere, yet all was tidy and the inmate was in her hammock by three."

It is this last gesture of yours that I put my faith in along with my own observations. We will expect you at Urania in two weeks' time.

Sincerely,
Mr. Dickens

· • ● • ·

A girl spins in circles on the cold stone floor. Far off, she is flying with the wild swans.

· • ● • ·

Days later, Ayre measures my height, waist, and feet and wraps a tape around my chest. Two weeks pass. And then, one evening, she brings me down to the basement tubs for a bath. Afterward, I comb my straight hair. It's grown to my chin since the last shearing. I beg Ayre not to cut it. She hesitates, then puts her scissors down.

"All right. But you must be sure to tuck your hair completely under your bonnet tomorrow so no one sees."

She presses a parcel into my hands. "For your leave-taking tomorrow morning."

"My old clothes?" I shudder to think of the blood.

"Those we burnt. You're to wear what's sent from Urania."

A smile tugs the corners of her lips for the very first time. Bet matrons are trained never to do this.

·· ● ··

Alone in my cell, I unwrap the parcel. A long green dress, the color of an evergreen forest! Thick and sturdy bombazine, woven to last! A wide bonnet with a green ribbon to match the dress! Brand-new undergarments! Tie-up boots of black leather! These I wiggle into at once, marveling at the precision of heel defining the stone floor with that ringing I had heard in the matrons' boots. All night long, those boots stay strapped to my feet.

Next morning, I awaken in the dark to dress. Twirling around, the hem of my dress spinning in circles, wishing for a mirror to see the girl in her new outfit. In a few minutes, I'll be out the gates, never to return. Now it's certain Emma won't find me here. She'll never know for sure about Tothill. I tuck her letter into my boot, taking it with me.

It's so early that the other girls have not yet gone down to the oakum factory. On my way out, at certain cell doors, Ayre slides each eyelet wide for me to look in and say my goodbyes. Cold silence rings in Hester's cell. Edwina lies quite still in her hammock and waves a pale hand. I whisper wishes at Rose's cell, hoping she will heal soon. Lines of a hymn, "Amazing Grace," fall from her lips, in rasping notes:

Amazing Grace, how sweet the sound
That saved a wretch like me.
I once was lost but now am found,
Was blind but now I see.

We circle to Ivy's cell last. Her brown eyes startle at the eyelet and then her fingers poke through. I grasp them hard. Her every thought, her every fear, shudders through me.

I have no one now. Jack's gone for good. I only had you for a time.

Ivy stretches her fingers out, touching my cheek with promises.

"Dear Orpha! How I wish to go with you to Urania. But they'd never want a girl like me. I'm a criminal. Bad as they come."

"You paid for what you did and your time will soon be over. That kind of life is behind you. You could begin again at Urania. Join me, Ivy! Tell the matron to write a letter for you."

Ayre nods for me to leave. Ivy's eyes shift, darkening.

"Don't forget me! I'll think of you always!"

My boots root to the floor by Ivy's cell door. Ayre slides her arm through mine and pulls me backward. Away. Between Ivy and me are now stone and empty space widening by the second. Throughout the tall hallway, my bosom friend's cries echo along the cold walls, bounce off the ceiling, magnifying.

"Or-pha! Or-pha! Or-pha!"

I only heard her voice a few times, mostly in a hurried whisper or a hiss. Always I wanted to hear more. There was never enough time for us to be together. Never enough time to tell her what happened to me, all the secrets I never spilled. I would have told them to her.

And then Ayre walks me down to the main floor, past the silent guards, for the last time. Fresh air fills the hallway. On the bottom step, beside Harred, stands a plump woman in a plain bonnet and broad cape. She steps forward.

"Miss Orpha Wood? I'm Mrs. Marchmont, the

matron in charge of Urania. Once I worked here at Tothill. It is my pleasure to take you to your new home now. Have you said your goodbyes?"

I nod and curtsy. Words get swallowed down my throat.

"Good," she says. "Then we'll ride there together right now."

Immediately she locks her elbow in mine, squeezing me tightly to her side, her body warm and solid, a tree trunk against my shivering. She guides me to the door. When it opens to the dawn's light, all time disappears as if I were never here at Tothill. Behind us, the iron door shuts and bolts. There, by the gate, a carriage waits.

Suddenly it hits me like a blast of March wind: out here, so close to the rookery, Luther still lives. He knew my every movement and exactly where to find me. He could sniff me out of any corner. Luther could pluck my thoughts as I thought them, turn them inside out and upside down.

My feet stop, drawing Urania's matron to a halt. My glance sweeps to all the dark corners of the prison on my left and right, then down the steps and onto the street. No one lurks here at this early hour. Likely, Luther is still sound asleep, in a drunken fog. The matron urges me forward.

It's odd how wobbly my legs are. I am a loose egg

without its shell. Above my head, buildings soar and morning fog presses upon everything. Pigeons flap their wings, swooping all around Tothill like a celebration. Out on the bustling street ahead, women aim their noses to the sky while men sneak bold glances my way. The greenness of my dress spreads around me like a vast field. My new boots click. They step ahead.

My Dear Miss Coutts,
February 27, 1857

As you have directed, I have sought recruits for Urania from Tothill Fields. So many girls are unsuitable there. Hester would be nothing but Trouble. Others, like Rose and Edwina, are doomed by their medical reports.

However, there is one Promising inmate who will most likely return to prostitution if we do not intervene. At present, Orpha Wood is secretive as they all are, and unwilling to face up to her crimes. To Miss Wood's credit, she reads and writes and has fine speech. What are the odds of a Literate lower class girl living in our society today? Fourteen in seventeen thousand!

Though her own family has Disowned her, I believe we can help by offering her another family. I am willing to take the chance and invite her to the Home on your behalf.

Ever Faithfully Yours,
CD

The carriage stops at a high brick house with a walled yard. Its door opens to loud voices and bright, swirling skirts. Sunshine blazes through sparkling windows, making my eyes smart. Laughter expands the room.

"Miss Wood, here you are, at last!" a thin young woman greets me. "I'm Miss Jane Macartney, assistant matron. Welcome to Urania Cottage."

Everything about her is quiet, from her dull brown-striped dress to her flat apron. As she approaches me, one foot trails slightly behind the other. She reaches out her hand, closing the space between us.

A girl in a lavender dress with flowing copper hair, like a hothouse flower in winter, her dark eyes very knowing, rushes over to clasp my hands too. She stops the breath in my chest.

"I'm Sesina. You'll get to know me very well. We're roommates. You will have a bang-up time with us, Orpha!"

She introduces the other girls standing nearby: curly-headed Fanny; Jemima, flat-faced, very tall, scrubbing the windows; Hannah pushing open the kitchen door beside a tiny girl named Alice; and Leah, hovering at the very edge of the girls, almost on tiptoe.

"How that green suits you! Sets off your eyes." Sesina looks me up and down, studying my dress. "Mr. Dickens has taste. He's the one who chose that color for you."

Hannah laughs. "Mr. Dickens insists on color. Nothing dull or drab like that Quaker uniform Miss Coutts wanted for us! To be made from plain brown derry, mind you!"

Then Fanny leans in close to whisper, "I've heard him say girls such as us who have led...ahem...forbidden lives...we have imagination. So color pleases us. Wouldn't you agree?"

She giggles, twirling in a teal dress cut like mine. Chatter fills the cottage with bright notes and ringing laughter. Fanny grabs my hand and pulls me around to show all the rooms upstairs and downstairs. The neatly made beds. Sun at the windows. A sparkling kitchen with big pots and pans. The cozy parlor. Hours later, we hear the matron call.

"Come now, girls." Mrs. Marchmont suddenly claps. "It's time for our dinner."

At once, all the girls rush to the table, surrounding

me on all sides. Amid their flushed faces, my plainness blares. They have grown their hair out, pinned it high in shiny waves, while mine is brittle, sticking up at odd angles. Beside them, my body is scoured flat as flint. As I lean over to pass the bread, mustiness drifts from beneath my dress: *Tothill!*

Pea soup is tasted to ringing compliments for the regular cook, Hannah, and today's bread maker, Alice, who rose before dawn to knead it. Rolls squish in my mouth, drowning in butter. Potatoes, baked in cream, are passed around. All the while, beer warms my belly. Like an anchor, my body sinks into a chair.

"You are replacing Agnes." Mrs. Marchmont turns to me. "She sailed to Australia a month ago with Polly. We all cried when our girls went aboard. Soon they will have jobs and a home."

Hannah mutters, "Hope they don't get seasick."

"Bet we'll hear 'em screaming all the way to London," Sesina says with a grin, "once they touch down on solid ground after sailing so long!"

All these girls seem like friends. Which ones will welcome me, I wonder. Whom to look out for, I'll know soon enough. No one could be truer than Ivy. If only I did not have to leave her there this morning, all alone. It already seems like yesterday. She would have been my bosom friend, I'm sure, just like Emma, if we had met elsewhere. *Both were sparks to my dead kindling. When we were together, their warmth heated my cold life.*

·· ● ··

After we clear the table, the matron beckons me to follow her. She has a way about her, straight-backed but not stiff, that says she is in charge. She shows me a timetable tacked on the wall.

"Part of your education here, Orpha, is learning how to keep a proper house. These are your new duties."

Chores can be ropes, something to climb; something to hold on to. I learned that at Tothill.

The timetable reads:

Orpha's daily duties: weeding potato beds, weeding and watering flowers in the back garden, chickens, keeping her own garden patch

> *Monday: dusting, dishes, washing clothes*
> *Tuesday: bread, dishes, airing of blankets and curtains*
> *Wednesday: soup for supper, soup for the poor, dishes*
> *Thursday & Friday: kitchen meals all day*
> *Saturday: full house scrubbing, dinner stew, soaking clothes*

I nod agreement as I sit down beside the matron. She is a large woman, nearing forty, with a wide bosom. Her hands and feet are broad as if capable of carrying any weight or doing all these chores herself. Mr. Dickens told me she is a widowed mother who raised three children on her own. That's why she came to work at Tothill. I shudder to think how deep that prison's ways may still run in her.

Then she points to a document. "Let's finish the last bit of business, shall we? You must sign your contract now."

I take a deep breath and scan it. The word *transportation* sits at the bottom where I have to sign my name.

The matron looks at me squarely. "Do you understand, Orpha, that once your education here is done, you will sail to one of the colonies? Most likely, you will never return to England."

England: my parents' bones resting in its dust; its memories seeded in my cells.

I nod and sign. *Give your own self away as you did before.*

·· ● ··

In the late afternoon, I meet Zachariah, Urania's gardener, handyman, and guard. Wrinkled and tattered as a scarecrow, cap in hand, he sways on his long, thin legs like beanpoles. It's a wonder he can stand up.

"Born right here in Shepherd's Bush, I was." The

old man grins a toothless smile. "It's a village named for shepherds who stopped here to rest before heading to London's Smithfield Market to sell their goods."

We stand high on Urania's back porch, the house solemn and three-storied behind us, as he points out long stretches of Miss Coutts's cornfields. There are few houses, mostly flat fields surrounding us. The cawing of crows makes me look up. Geese and pigeons swarm the air, so thick in number, their wings beat overhead with a swishing sound.

"Go on out and see the garden!"

Zachariah leaves me alone in the yard. All around, a high fence hems it so no one sees in. There is a locked gate too.

Luther can't get at me here or ever guess where I am hidden. Miles and miles stretch between us now.

The garden is still mostly sleeping, bowed into its brown with hints of green poking up. There is sky and birdflight here; sunlight warming my body; all on my own, not tethered to other girls. Stone no longer surrounds me, only soft earth. If I press my boot heel down, it gives.

It's my birthday month, although I've told no one. At seventeen, this surprising gift appears: *a refuge!*

Dare I spin in circles, head back, eyes on the setting sun? I do. Above my head, the whole sky opens wide.

·· ● ··

How odd to enter a bedroom where I am not alone. Instead, I have two roommates: Leah and Sesina.

At once, Sesina pries me with questions. "You from Tothill? Never been there but one of my boyfriends has. Whatever were you in there for?"

Leah jabs her. "Sesina, you know the rules."

"Rules be damned! You know all about me and I know all there is to know about you too," Sesina retorts. "Good that I do. Don't I comfort you when you cry? It's 'cause I know your story."

Leah flushes and turns her head away. "Don't!"

Sesina tosses her curls, sits down at the mirrored dresser, and twists strips of cloth around the ends of her coppery hair. She glares at Leah's image in the mirror, then shifts her gaze right onto me. Her eyes are direct, like darts.

·· ● ··

Next morning, I awake to Sesina singing a counting rhyme, propped high above me, her hair hanging in my face:

> Eaver, weaver, chimney sweeper,
> Had a wife but couldn't keep her.
> Had another, didn't love her,
> Up the chimney he did shove her!

"Finally! The inmate is awake. Dead to the world she has been."

Leah peeks over Sesina's shoulder, her cheeks sucked tight.

"Let's give her *our* rules, Leah. Five minutes to dress before we go downstairs to prayer."

Sesina leans closer, her curls brushing my nose, her dark eyes framed by thick lashes.

"First, Dickens's rule—we make up one another's bed each morning and check for anything hidden. Such as..." She tosses her hair. "Gin. Cigarettes. What girl doesn't like those things? So if you find any of my treasures, dear Orpha, you won't report them, will you?"

Her chin edges closer, touching mine. I twist away from her.

"Is that a yes?"

I nod.

"Good!" Sesina lets go, bounces off the bed, and shoos me away so she can make it up.

·· ● ··

Prayers mark each morning and end each evening. Hester's sneering voice reminds me, "He'll shove God down your throat like all the rest!"

·· ● ··

Mornings, for our first lesson, we recite the alphabet and then afterward copy it. Cards are passed around with paintings of objects. One of a "Kangaroo" in the colonies says they are "good-tempered." Some Urania girls can read only a few words. While Hannah and Leah read books, Fanny stabs letters onto her slate, curses bubbling out of her mouth with each stroke: "Fuckers!"

Our instructor, Miss Macartney, stands behind me, hair smoothed into a bun, straight white teeth, and her dress seams falling perfectly. She looks over my shoulder. Her low voice strikes a pleased tone.

"Write what you wish, Orpha. You don't need my lessons."

The slate fills with words stretching into sentences:

Here the sky is everywhere peeking into the house. Anytime I am free, I can run out to the garden to see the sun reveal tight buds on the trees.

Words paint pictures the moment you write them down. *Who am I writing to? The missing ones: Pa; Ivy; Emma.*

From her chair beside me, Fanny gasps. "Are those real *words*?"

When I nod, she shakes her head. "I can't do it nohow."

"All the girls write letters home to Urania, I heard." I set my hand upon hers to widen her *B*. "You will too."

"Show me how," she begs. "So's I don't look the idiot."

Back and forth we go, from my slate to hers. My words and her wobbly letters, one at a time. Sometimes she stamps her foot when she makes a silly mistake. I almost laugh at the fuss she makes.

But then she leans close to whisper, "I never held a book before I came here. Or a quill. On my contract, I jotted an *X*, the one letter I learned at that bloody Magdalen Hospital. They never let me forget my past. To them, I was a sinner. So I refused to learn anything from them."

Suddenly I remember the morning they brought me to Tothill. *It will swallow me whole*, I thought, *I won't ever find my way out.*

I look into Fanny's startled blue eyes. "Once you know your letters, they'll be your friends."

"I can't do it, I tell you. It don't make no sense."

"But you do know some already. Like *F* and *Y*, letters of your very own name." My hand over hers, I guide her fingers to write *Fanny*. She leans close to admire it.

The girl named Jemima tosses her head of thick black curls and scowls.

·· ● ··

Time here is divided into little bits much like at Tothill. It is meant to tame girls like us.

This afternoon, we learn to knit a lace shawl from a pattern named Survival. The silky yellow yarn, soft as a cat's belly, must be worked in an exact pattern or else is full of holes from dropped stitches and must be yanked out and begun again. Thirty times I've done it already.

In the corner, the assistant matron, Miss Macartney, knits too. Every so often, her eyes rest on each girl as if deciding something about us. She only speaks when she must. She doesn't chatter like all the rest. Mrs. Marchmont leads the lesson. She lifts the yarn high above her head, turning it in the sunlight, as if it were a precious jewel, then holds it against Fanny's dress to show how the yellow brightens the teal color. Fanny claps. The matron smiles at this. She demonstrates how to knit on one side of the shawl and purl on the other; to wrap yarn around the needle, making new stitches to form the lace; then to knit stitches together to decrease.

My yarn crisscrosses. Held to the light, it is full of holes like cheese chewed by mice. Jemima roars.

"Give it here!" she shouts, yanking out all my stitches.

She begins it again, showing me how to stab with the needle in front of the yarn for the knit side and behind for the purl side. "Move in and around, Orpha. One from the front. One from the backside."

Jemima bites her lips, elbows Fanny, and both giggle, their cheeks flushing bright.

The matron is dead silent. Her assistant matron immediately stops knitting. They stare straight at Jemima and Fanny. Both girls drop their heads to their work. I am handed the needles again while Fanny guides my clumsy fingers. It takes long minutes, breath held, to finish one row without mistakes. Three perfect rows take up all the time before supper. But something amazing begins to happen to the yarn. Little bumps line up where I decreased. Nearby, tiny holes open to become lace.

"Take it slow. A stitch at a time." Alice's voice squeaks from across the room. "It ain't a race."

DICKENS'S CASE BOOK

What shall I say to Miss Coutts about keeping poor Alice on? The girl has surpassed the time we agreed to keep her. Any placement would welcome her but she is not yet fit. Reverend Illingworth will certainly back me up; he was the one who found her starving in his parish after her stay at Coldbath.

"A Pure girl," he recommended her. "Never Corrupted." And so she is. But Miss Coutts has the final say. It is her funds that keep our girls at Urania.

CD

Days pass. Three girls are chosen to accompany the matron on an outing to town. Mrs. Marchmont invites me, linking her arm in mine as she did the day we met. I shake my head and pull away. How can I be seen out in the world after Tothill? With a shout, Fanny springs up to join them instead.

When the girls return, they burst through the door laughing, cheeks reddened, mouths chewing caramel and bonbons. Whiffs of butter and chocolate and fresh air rush into the cottage with them. They fling their shawls off, spinning around. They seem to have visited another world.

·· ● ··

We gather in the parlor evenings to knit and embroider our alphabet samplers until bedtime prayer. Alice is excused. She's a fine needlewoman, as that was her trade, though she made little money. She leans forward, stroking the pages of the book on her lap, *The Child's Fairy Library*. Such a spell she's under. She hasn't said a word for a full hour. Of all the girls, she's the quietest as well as the palest.

Miss Macartney, who says I can call her Miss Jane, reads aloud to us from Herman Melville's *The Whale*. It's very somber. Almost like the Bible. Full of dread. Something terrible will happen, you can feel it. Yet Fanny yawns during the reading and Sesina rolls her eyes. When the hour is done, Miss Jane excuses herself to work on Urania's accounts.

"I would never want to meet a man such as Captain

Ahab," jokes Leah. "Got his mind on such a silly thing—a whale named Moby-Dick that keeps swimming away!"

Sesina laughs. "Luckily, most men have their mind on other things."

"Stop talking nonsense!" Jemima jerks her head my way. "We'd better teach this new girl the ropes. Wait till she finds out we're checked here like schoolgirls."

"Oh, you're mad as hops 'cause you lost your marks this week but I still got mine," boasts Sesina. "I know how to play the game."

They begin explaining the system of earning marks for good behavior, and how every day we are judged on such things as Truthfulness.

"Imagine *you* telling no lies about yourself!" Sesina throws back her head and points. From across the room, Jemima glowers.

"Industry. Temper," Hannah calls out like a song.

"Oh, Jemima, you are out!" screeches Fanny. "Again!"

"Propriety of Conduct. Conversation," Sesina mocks.

"I never was good at those." Pale Alice turns to me. "Sesina's the one with the gift of gab. And Hannah too."

"Temperance—that one is very hard on a girl." Fanny frowns. Then she pinches her nose, making a high, squeaking voice to recite, "Or-der! Punc-tu-al-i-ty! E-con-o-my! Clean-li-ness!"

"Not my cup of tea." Jemima frowns as she knits. "That's Hannah's line, through and through."

Leah smiles. "We get checks for doing well. And use them to buy things we want, like wool to knit mittens or Sesina's tortoiseshell hair clip. We earn a wage too that gets banked until we emigrate."

"But we can lose them fast! If we cuss, fight, or are cheeky to the matron, they're gone"—Fanny snaps her fingers—"just like that!"

It's then I remember that for the first months in Urania, I will be on trial. One wrong move and they could boot me out.

The click of Jemima's needles draws my attention back.

"…Saturday evenings," Hannah is saying, "the matron shows us her book where she's tallied our marks. I keep my own book too to make sure I get what's coming to me."

"We all keep score, Hannah!" Jemima's voice booms. "What else in bloody hell have we got to do here?"

Once a month, they tell me next, are committee meetings with the clergyman Reverend Illingworth, Dr. Brown, Mr. Dickens, our matron, and Mr. Chesterson, the governor of Coldbath Prison.

Jemima frowns. "They call us in one by one to ask how we are doing. They have already discussed us, for we had our ears flat to their door, listening. So why do they put us through such nonsense?"

Fanny clears her throat as if to spit. "My whole life I've been judged. Why, even those blasted matrons at Coldbath sneaked up to the eyelet just for a peep at me. Many a time, I was tempted to poke their eyes out. Or show them my bare arse. But if I did, I'd still be locked up in there right now, wouldn't I?"

Giggles fill the parlor.

"Do what we all do when called in to them, Orpha." Sesina winks. "Keep your hands behind your back and your eyes on your boots. They won't know what the hell to think of you!"

.. ● ..

It's late. Metal sings against metal, a sound so familiar I once counted time by it. Keys! I tiptoe to the landing. Below, Mrs. Marchmont is walking across the dining room, her keys jingling like a Tothill matron as she turns the many locks of the back door.

Her low voice travels. "I've begun to worry about him, Jane. Ever since he confided in me that if he scaled the highest mountains in Switzerland, it would offer him no relief!"

"Mr. Dickens works much too hard," Miss Jane answers. "He seems compelled. Lately, he looks as if he hasn't slept at all!"

I tiptoe back to my room. It is pitch dark. Shivers sizzle up my spine remembering. Luther always knew the exact time to come: when I was sleeping. Up and down the crowded rookery, no one heard my cries through the fist jammed in my mouth.

Inside our room, Leah curls up fernlike on her side, her face wet with tears. Sesina lies on her back studying the ceiling, sucking her nails.

The night is sleepless.

SEVEN

Jemima corners me in the long hallway between the kitchen and front hall, blocking my way. Her look is pure Tothill: narrowed eyes and a sneer. If she were an alley cat, her rear end would be raised high.

"You come from Tea Garden, don't ya? Tothill girls are all ladybirds. Do it for money. In the street. Or in the sewers. They're all diseased. Priggin' is much cleaner. I've lifted everything I ever needed. Got by without any man."

My hands shoot out like a tigress's claws, jagged nails nearing her upturned face. But she is quicker. Her hands grab hold of mine and twist my wrists hard. My boot smacks her shin. Footsteps bang, coming from the kitchen. Mrs. Marchmont slips into the space between us, her big bosom heaving.

"Oh, girls, it's so good you are having a conversation. Friendship is what we like to encourage here. For now, though, Orpha has chores outside. Would you care to join her there, Jemima?"

Jemima gathers her skirts. "No, ma'am, I got dustin' to do."

"Well, then, this evening in the parlor, you can continue your little talk." The matron straightens her back. "I'll be sure to listen in."

I walk away gulping breaths.

·· ● ··

Zachariah finally joins me in the garden. He'd been too busy to teach me, he says. Now we head to the chicken coop, where it seems I will be in charge. My bet is no one else wants to do it. Jemima turned it down in a hurry. From inside the coop, the loud and insistent racket of clucking chickens greets me.

"They'll settle down soon as you feed 'em. It's that one you must look out for." Zachariah points to a stringy black-and-white rooster with a bright red comb on his head. "Stay clear of him! A purebred Doring! Full of fire, he is. He's Richard the Third and he hates girls. He'll fly right up at you and tear your hair out."

Richard squints at me sharply, shifting from claw to claw on his perch. The gardener shoos him out the door with the end of a broomstick. One by one, all the hens follow the rooster in a straight line. Hidden deep in the straw, I find eggs blue, white, speckled, and brown. Afterward, we scrape the roosts clean of manure and cover them in fresh straw.

"Overseas, you'll have your own chickens to care for. Eggs and meat aplenty," Zachariah says. "Maybe our matron will teach you the knack of wringing their necks for soup. She does it so quick—in a blink, they're dead!"

I scatter slops on the ground and pour water. Some hens are beauties, like the hen whose feathers are freckled with specks of brown as if deliberately painted. Zachariah says she's Cornish. A white hen flings dirt as she digs, shoving the others. Richard lands with a flurry of wings. I step back at once. There's a chorus of tutting. Such squawking! It sounds rather like complaints and gossip about who got what to eat.

How like Urania's girls they are! Fluffed up and chattering in the parlor. Suddenly, a sound pops out of my mouth. It shakes my belly and shoulders hard. Laughter, of all things!

So fitting they have put me in charge of the chickens.

·· ● ··

After supper, the matron beckons Jemima away from our sewing circle with a stern look, like a flash of Tothill. There's something steely about Mrs. Marchmont, although she has not been unkind. Not yet. My needle jabs my finger as I watch them talking. Jemima returns, eyeing me darkly, muttering low curses.

"Orpha?" Mrs. Marchmont calls me out next. She looks exactly as she did with Jemima, somber and unsmiling.

"Can you guess why I wish to speak with you now?"

"Yes, ma'am." I curtsy. "It's about Jemima."

"It's about *you* and Jemima. We don't accept fighting of any sort at Urania. If you have a problem with another girl, you must come directly to me first. Is that clear?"

I nod.

"I want you to have a fine start here, Orpha. Since this is your first incident, I will not report it to Mr. Dickens. However, if you persist with this behavior, then I must also tell of this indiscretion. All marks will be lost."

Perhaps I gasp. Tears make my eyes smart. Before I know it, the matron sets her hand on my shoulder. No one has done that since Emma.

"Stay away from Jemima. She's a troubled girl. Let's hope both of you will do well here."

· · ● · ·

"Those were real pearls sewn into her hat. Ostrich feathers too!"

Afterward, as I slip into the parlor again, Sesina is describing upper-class ladies promenading the streets of London with hat boxes and packages carried by servants and footmen in tow. The center of attention, Sesina squawks loud and bright as a parrot while I cling to the walls like dust. Didn't the others at Tothill warn me? Urania is not a refuge. One false move and they could kick me out—all because of Jemima. If I fail here, I'll be out on the streets of the rookery: *his* prey.

Luther's face has been flashing all day. An urge pokes me to look over my shoulder, in case he hears I am here. Those greasy lips that smothered mine before I knew what a man's kiss was. My fists clench, threatening to smash something. All day, my feet have been itching to pace. Outside, where the light is fading, where the fence is high and the gate is locked tight, no one will find me. I must run him off. *Will they let me just go outside on my own, without asking, without permission?*

I slip out to pace the yard. No one follows. In a circular bed of herbs, I kneel, rubbing my fingers against newly coiled leaves of spearmint, bee balm and lemon balm, just like in our own kitchen garden of long ago, tended by Pa and then by me. The scent of lemon and sharp mint fills the air.

As I drop to the ground, a sound heaves from my belly in a high keening note, like the call of a soaring hawk.

All at once I've descended into the rookery with Luther.

He jabbed it flat and cold against my throat. *Feel this knife? You bloody well won't tell.* That was the first time.

My fists pound the sodden ground and my feet kick up dirt. The times I shrank from his huge body and found no hiding place. All the while, the one that was Orpha—the child who could play and sing—died. The man who grabbed her stole my soul. There's no one to tell me how to get it back. For I have never told, and never will, exactly what he did to me.

I roll onto my back. All around, the white rim of fence encircles the yard like strong arms. *No one can get in here*, I remind myself. Far above me shine the million dots of silvery stars. Through London's smog, I rarely saw a single star.

This is what I imagined Urania would be: a home of space and stars. A refuge where I could be free to run outside just as I did when I was a child, playacting in the dark, pretending to be anyone I wished to be.

From the porch, Miss Jane shouts my name. As I run to her, her face lights up. She's the kind of person who lives in the background like a minor character in a play, highlighting the others, never taking center stage. As we head inside, my step slowing to match hers, how I wish she were Ivy calling me in, calling me home.

"There's so much for you to learn here." Her voice is calm and slow, like smoke to bees. "And you will heal. As I myself did."

"You...did?" I stare at her. Even with her limp, she moves with certainty and stillness.

She nods. "Someday, I will tell you of it. I believe it *is* possible, *very* possible, that a girl as young as you are can go on, in spite of everything."

That lights up my mind for days. Every so often, I think of what she said, pulling those words out like medicine to soothe a wound.

DICKENS'S CASE BOOK

It is already halfway through the month and I have yet to visit Urania other than through Correspondence that flies back and forth between Mrs. Marchmont and myself, often daily. The widowed matron, as capable and kind as the day I first hired her, is still no match for the tricks of the Virgin Charges.

You could lose yourself in those girls. Untamed as stray Kittens.

CD

One evening in the parlor, we work on our tasks: knitting, embroidery, hemming, drawing, or reading. Alice demonstrates a smooth running stitch for the hem of a sky-blue dress, which will be mine to wear once done. It's the color of innocence, of virgins. The Virgin Mary wore a dress of such a shade.

Mrs. Marchmont has been bustling from task to task

while we sew. She's always in motion, her plump face flushed. Now she falls breathless into a chair to read aloud from *Sidney's Emigrant's Journal*. The ladies' column is the girls' favorite part and they beg to hear it again and again, bringing a smile to the matron's lips. The journal talks about how good husbands can be found in Australia and how "in the towns there is as much gaiety as in England." Rather more!

Sesina smirks at that last part. The others discuss husbands.

"What if a suitor in Australia asks about our life in London?" Alice wonders, pulling my threads out yet again. "What shall we say?"

Fanny lifts her head. "What if they find out who I was before?"

The matron's voice rises. "Girls, you know that once you go to the colonies, you must keep your past to yourself. That is the rule. You must act as if it never happened. That's what Mr. Dickens advises."

"Mum's the word!" Jemima mutters, knitting rows of her shawl.

Then Fanny asks, "But ain't anyone fearful of leaving England and going to the ends of the earth?"

Leah calls from the kitchen. "Ma'am, kitchen's clean! Miss Jane's ordering supplies. She's asking if you need to add anything."

The matron puts her magazine down. "We'll continue later, girls."

Crossing the room, she suddenly stops. "Come now, Alice, you've worked long enough. Go to bed this instant. Tomorrow's another day."

Alice looks up from her sewing, the circles beneath her eyes dark as storm clouds. She pushes her hands on the arms of the chair to help herself stand, then slowly trudges upstairs.

"Ever seen the hulks?" Sesina whispers as soon as the matron is out of earshot. "Ships waiting on the Thames jammed with convicts waiting for transportation. The Floating Academy, they call it. That's who you'll be meeting in Australia. Thieves! Murderers! Rapists! They'll swarm the place. It's them that'll bring all the gaiety."

I have seen the men on those ships. Filthy as beasts. Lined up shoulder to shoulder like stinking animals. Their shouts and curses travel to shore. Some are even murdered on board. If ever there was a fitting prison for Luther, it would be there.

"If Mr. Dickens were here right now"—Sesina turns to me—"you'd have to tell him everything once he caught that look on your face. Penny for your thoughts, Orpha!"

Words freeze in my throat.

"Been to see Dickens yet?" Fanny asks. "The man's

a force of nature. A blizzard, I tell you! He can move people. He got us all here, didn't he? If only I'd met him sooner. He'd have knocked my Jed down a notch or two."

"I told him things I never dared tell nobody." Hannah nods.

Sesina looks up. "Why that Dickens wants to hear such stories, I'll never know. You should see his quill fly when I give him juicy tidbits about my boyfriends."

Giggles circle around the room. "Tell us some!" Fanny begs.

Sesina tells about a boyfriend who kissed her hair and fondled it for hours in ecstasy, sniffing it with deep groans and sighs, falling to his knees and keeping her waiting for a single kiss.

"Such worship!" Sesina crosses her legs, rocking them back and forth, with a satisfied smile.

Hannah sighs. "Don't you think it weighs on Dickens, though? He comes in all buttoned up in his crisp white shirt and stiff jacket. But when he leaves, he sags like an old man."

"That man is hell-bent on getting something out of me." Jemima sets her lips flat. "And he's not getting one word."

·· ● ··

Like a chess piece, men have marked my every move. Mr. Dickens is small and bristles with unknown purpose.

His sharp eyes sliced, yet how they lingered: clay for him to mold.

·· ● ··

The next afternoon, when Mr. Dickens enters the Home, his presence is felt at once. Backs straighten. Hands flatten skirts smooth. All murmurs cease. The matron summons me to the back parlor, where Mr. Dickens waits.

At once, he begins the interview. "Welcome to Urania, Miss Wood. I want to complete a case history of your life so we know best how to guide you over the next months. Let's get started, shall we?"

Jemima is right. The man tracks a scent like a hound on the hunt. Mr. Dickens removes a maroon leather-bound book, thick as a Bible, from where it is kept under lock and key inside a glass cabinet and flips it open. At his right elbow are quills, all with sharp tips, and a bottle of dark blue ink. He fingers one quill after another, examining each with a critical eye.

Now he dips one. "What kind of work did you first do?"

"Theater, sir. The one my pa directed. I fetched costumes for his actors, even played at dressing for the part all on my own. Each costume had a speech and a story to tell: the ivory Cornelia gown; the Fool's jiggling coxcomb; and a sparkly headdress fit for a queen. For hours, I listened to the actors' voices lifting from the stage.

When it was my turn to step onto the stage, my costume was like a charm."

"Did other children work there also?"

The long, snow-white goose feather sails across the paper. Short dabs into the inkpot without a turn of his head.

"Only the daughter of the man who owned the theater. She rigged curtains and set the stage."

"Her name?"

My breath catches. "Emma."

To name is to conjure: across the gangplank, hands outstretched to catch me, the daring in her dark eyes burning like fire. "Leap!" she yelled. And so I did.

Mr. Dickens looks up at once. "What happened to her?"

All the breath leaves me then. *Her heart-shaped face reddened from crying, her wave frozen in the air as I was dragged away.*

"That last time I saw Emma, Pa had just died and I was whisked to the workhouse. I never saw her again."

"Would you wish to see your friend again, Miss Wood?"

The question stands in the air between us as if it had feet. Her letter is tucked between the wooden slats of the chicken coop, safe from prying eyes. How many times have I read it? Countless!

"Someday. If I felt proper again."

He scans my cheeks, where the blood pumps hard. His pen lifts.

"Tell me about the workhouse next."

"I was sent there to pay my father's drink debt after he died. Every day, I worked with a gang of children under charge of two horrid old men called the Barclays."

"What kind of work?"

I grit my teeth. "The Barclays led us to the banks of the Thames where the sewage pipes leaked out so we could scoop up circles of fat floating on top and set it upon a cork, rolling it round and round to make a ball of fat. Its stink was awful."

The river appears before me. Bitter cold drilled into my hands as I grabbed the slimy fat, feet sliding down the muddy bank. Never far from the nudge of a boot at my back if I didn't work quick enough.

"Do you know what they did with this...material?"

"Why, sir, they called it mud butter. The workhouse sold it for soap and candles and to thicken bread. And also to make butter. Mild Dorset Butter. I could never eat it after that."

Mr. Dickens holds his quill in midair like an exclamation point. I stop talking and can't go on. I never told this story to anyone. Not even my aunt or uncle knew of it. That was the place where my tears ran into the reeking Thames, joining the filth from the sewers.

A dreadful idea twists in my mind—what Mr. Dickens hears will sway him to let me stay or make me go. My lips press together as I clutch the bottom of my chair. I've already decided what to do with Mr. Dickens since the day we met: hide my past like Jemima and never let it loose.

DICKENS'S CASE BOOK: NUMBER 98

As usual, Miss Wood shuts tight as an Oyster shell. Shifting into secrecy in some dark underwater Refuge as soon as I steer her toward some facts. No doubt she is hiding much of her story.

She serves her words to me on a Pauper's plate. I shall persist.

CD

Mornings, upon awakening, images brew in a fog of dreams, thick and slow. Sometimes I'm walking Old Pye Street, calling Pa's name with no answer. Then the corner appears, where Luther could always find me. My bloated belly flashes, and I am running through the labyrinthine alleys away from him.

On the day I passed the brothel that winter, I was

stone cold from sleeping in the graveyard. So I stepped inside, begging for a bite to eat and a touch of warm. The women eyed my belly and felt it, telling me that a baby was surely coming, just as my aunt had accused me of. *You'll do.* They nodded. *To cook and clean here.* So I stayed on for two months. They said a man came around once. *One to watch out for,* they warned. *Looking for a young girl that ran away, one named Orpha. Couldn't be you, could it?*

I never dared give them my real name. And so I pushed brooms, brewed tea, and cooked soup. There were girls there younger than me, faces pinked and eyes circled in kohl. Older ones with rose-petaled lips, the flesh of their bosoms exposed. Some with purpled eyes. Another who coughed all day and night. And the madam, who called out loudly, awakening me at dawn when the women's work was all done.

"Gimme my black drops, child, lord knows I need 'em!" She reached out her trembling hand to open the bottle, releasing the scent of nutmeg into the air.

The day I ran from there was the day they caught me.

·· ● ··

We take turns pressing our ears to the closed back parlor door after the trustees march inside for the committee meeting. Hannah keeps Miss Jane busy in the kitchen with endless babbling. Inside, Mr. Dickens is speaking.

"I know what you're going to tell me—that I'm being

extravagant again. But I want those parlor curtains replaced. Since Urania opened eleven years ago, they've faded. I've spotted emerald moiré in a shop and bargained for it. Alice will sew it up. Agreed?"

"Dickens, you always find a way to get what you want," booms a deep voice.

"If only I could transform a girl as easily as a curtain, Dr. Brown!"

Laughter fills the room. Hands bang on the table. The men are so near, I can picture them clearly.

"Shall we continue?" The matron clears her throat. "On the subject of Jemima!"

"What's Sticky Fingers up to now?" Dickens roars loudly.

"That temper of hers! She insulted Hannah's delicious lamb stew. Kicked the door of her room when banned from the table. As of this week, she has no marks left."

"Give her warning. If she doesn't earn marks this week, tell Sticky Fingers she's on trial and can't stay on. That might rouse her."

Another voice joins in, cutting and loud. "You knew she was borderline when we took her in."

Dickens sighs. "Against my better judgment, I brought her here, Chesterson. She was headed straight back to the streets otherwise. I'd give her a month before she was caught stealing again."

"We'll reassess whether she's made progress at our next meeting," Chesterson responds. "I'll vote her out if she hasn't."

"How is Alice faring?" asks someone else. "Miss Coutts is letting her stay on past her time. I am grateful for that."

"Too quiet, Reverend Illingworth." The matron tuts. "I caught her lying on her bed, muffling coughs in her pillow. She's still recuperating."

Dickens's voice again. "Once the Little Mouse gets over the consumption, off she goes to a warmer climate. Better for her lungs. And Hedgehog seems to be doing rather well in the kitchen, I must say. It's the perfect den for her. Now call in the new one."

With one step into that room, facing those stares and all that silence, it seems I am back at Tothill. I slide my hands behind my back and curtsy. My eyes find my boots and stay fixed there.

"This is Miss Wood." The matron introduces me. "She is fitting into our routines nicely. She not only knows her letters but is coaxing our girls to learn them too. You've been a big help to us, Orpha."

I curtsy again.

"How do you like Urania, Miss Wood?" asks Dr. Brown.

"It's . . . very good, sir."

"Is there anything in particular that you enjoy here?"

If one of the girls had asked, a long list would have fallen from my mouth: the new green leaves, every meal, my sky-blue dress in the making, even Richard the Third. But all I can squeeze out is "Everything, sir."

I keep my eyes on my boots. They are scuffed and need shining. Throat clearing and silence fill the room.

"Well, fine then. You may return to your work," Dr. Brown mutters. "And do have those boots polished next time we meet."

I shut the door tight and lean in with Fanny. The men's groans echo in our ears.

"Why they all suddenly grow quiet and humble when they come into this room, may the devil tell me!" exclaims Chesterson. "They keep their hands behind them, a sure sign of holding back."

"Even the new one does it, as if they belong to some kind of club!" the deep voice of Dr. Brown protests.

The two of us rush away as fast as our boots can go, Fanny's curls bouncing, hands over our mouths. Laughter threatens to explode from our lungs. We stop to breathe out in a roar that bursts loose at the other end of the house.

·· EIGHT ··

I awaken in a pool of hot stickiness. Blood soaks the bleached white sheets. Deep in my belly, there's a heartbeat of cramps.

"Didn't you guess it was coming?"

Sesina slides her eyes my way as she gathers the sheets for soaking, her eyebrows rising.

She's the one I want to ask. But I can't tell her or anybody else, least of all Mr. Dickens. A girl doesn't speak to a man of that.

Perhaps they did not sew me up as they swore they did. And Luther did not finish me as I believed he did.

·· • ··

From the top floor of the cottage, there is a view of draft horses plowing the fields, farmers following behind, shouting. In their wake, boys gather stones into baskets. Their work begins at dawn and continues as I dust, wash windows, and carry laundry from the line. Long after supper the men's yells echo far across the fields.

Each day, the sun's rays shine stronger and deeper yellow. They stretch farther into the rooms, awakening me earlier. After breakfast, while we learn arithmetic lessons, the parlor beams with sharp spring light.

To watch Sesina then can take your breath away. She sits exactly where the morning sun spreads long rays through the eastern windows, sighing into her chair and lifting her glowing coppery head from a page of sums to smile at the sun as if it were her secret lover. She cranes her neck like a sleek cat to stare past the fence into the street that leads to London.

There are questions I want to ask her. Sesina will be the one to know, the only one who'd dare say such things. There will be a price to pay if I ask.

·· ● ··

We sit for morning lessons. On the parlor wall hangs Alice's embroidered sampler, a garden of colors. It's a record sewn of all the letters and numbers we must learn. Alice's *B* is bold in red thread; *M* marches in mourning black; and *N* trembles like a dancer in pale pink on pointed feet.

My head is bowed as I read. Words in a book are a cave to fall into. But there are no words for what happened. It can never be told. For it occupies all of me. Once it comes over me, nothing else is real.

"Miss Wood?"

Mrs. Marchmont must have been calling my name to announce the end of the reading lesson. The other girls' heads are already bowed to their sums. Fanny is counting out loud on her fingers.

Suddenly Jemima explodes. "Why the hell do we have to learn division? What bloody difference will it make once we're in that cursed shithole Australia? It's full of bastards anyhow!"

Her words clap like black thunderbolts across the room.

"Quite a sauce-box that girl is!" Hannah teases.

The matron frowns. "That's quite enough, Jemima! Five marks lost for swearing. No more warnings! Your score is now in the minus. Mr. Dickens will be informed at once. You are officially on trial."

Her voice has a Tothill edge to it: ice and knives.

Jemima throws her slate to the floor and stomps off. I am sure I hear the word *fuck* slam like an axe from her lips.

.. ● ..

Hannah, our cook, is waiting for us in the kitchen. She is hefty, with a round belly, pink-skinned as a piglet.

The matron pats her shoulder. "Hannah will teach you how to make healthful food from practical recipes. In London, progressive women are following the advice of Mrs. Beeton. She publishes a column about cooking and running a household."

"Beeton calls this beef and barley soup recipe we're making today 'Useful Soup for Benevolent Purposes.'"

Hannah grins. "Who wouldn't want to make soup with such a holy name?"

Mrs. Marchmont nods. "Every Wednesday, after cooking for Urania, Hannah sets aside a pot for the poor. We feed many mouths and keep costs low with these recipes. That's what Mrs. Beeton promotes."

With one hand, the cook stirs; the other wipes the counter. Beneath each foot is a rag she swirls whenever she steps. The floor is polished to a sheen.

"Hannah's secret is"—the matron smiles as she leaves us—"she cleans as she cooks and pays attention to everything she does."

Hedgehog! That's what Mr. Dickens called Hannah. It's the perfect nickname. Instead of digging, she wipes. She's not his pet, though. Alice is. He defended her being allowed to stay on.

The cook now sets supper china in piles, counting each pile twice.

"Suppose you're wondering what I'm doing. It's counting. I learned to count long before Clerkenwell. There I counted plenty. The strands of oakum I untwisted. Every speck of dust floating in the oakum room. Now, that's an impossible task, I tell you!"

The cook does not take a breath. "I know I'm a church bell, my voice always ringing." She frowns. "I'm always mumbling numbers too. Mrs. Marchmont says she's seen it before. It somehow makes me feel safe to count. So I do it."

She scans the kitchen floor, pleased with its shine.

I edge my words in quickly. "I daydream...when I can."

Hannah nods her curly head. "At any moment, your life can change. So you must pin time flat. That's why I count...So let's start cooking our 'Useful and Benevolent Beef and Barley Soup.' Our only purpose is to eat it tonight. Take a look in this pot."

"It's just cold water. Nothing else!"

"That's how you begin—with fresh cold water from the well. Now we'll add these four pounds of beef trimmings with all the big bones and two pounds of barley. Then boil it until the beef falls apart. You get all the vitamins out of the meat that way."

She lines up carrots next with turnips, onions, celery, herbs, and leeks all in straight rows, counting them twice.

"You need to chop these vegetables with a knife so sharp, it can split hairs." Hannah grins.

Indeed, she demonstrates this, yanking a strand of her own hair and slicing straight through it. Over an hour later, when steam blows out of the pot, Hannah peeks in.

"Good! The beef is softening. Now dump those

vegetables in and let them boil another hour. My soup recipe not only tastes good but is more nutritious too. I'm going to write Mrs. Beeton and tell her so."

She points to *The Englishwoman's Domestic Magazine* on the table, where she's been reading recipes by Mrs. Beeton.

Whatever can't be used in the soup pot is scooped into a pail: blackened potatoes, carrot peelings, yellowed herbs. This mess of slops is for my chickens.

Just as I'm headed out the back door, Hannah stops me.

"Want to know what happened to me? Dickens did. When I was eight, I saw my ma stabbed to death by my father. Dickens says such things stick to you forever. Told me to talk about it to set it free. But talking hasn't done the job so far. So I count."

It could have happened to me too.

He saw your eyes click to the door just as he stepped into the shadows where you hid, your feet already lifting to scoot away. At once, he drew the Valentin out of its sheath, testing its pointed tip and razor-sharp edges with his fingertip. "No matter where you poke it, it mars."

I wanted to ask Hannah when I'd forget my past, but it wouldn't have done any good. She hasn't found a way either.

·· ● ··

When they catch sight of me with the slop pail later that afternoon, the hens circle me. I squat down, flinging scraps around. After their meal, the freckled hen hops onto my lap, thinking it a nest. I've spied feathers like hers in fancy hats. Freckles, I name her, petting her smooth back.

Richard flies in screeching and slides to a landing with sharp claws to viciously shred a prized potato peel. The girls are so in awe of him; they hop back, clucking in low tones to peck at Richard's leavings.

Tomorrow I shall sneak bread crumbs into my pockets just for the hens. Richard the Third won't get a nibble. The chore holds my feet down to this soft earth, Urania.

·· ● ··

On Saturday, the windows are flung wide open. Curtains are pulled down and soaked in barrels. All morning, Fanny and I whirl through the bottom floor springcleaning, pushing furniture away from the walls, sweeping behind. We don't leave an inch untouched by our dust rags. Mr. Dickens is expected within days.

"The Chief Inspector will check each and every corner, mark my word," Fanny warns. "There'll be hell to pay should he find one tiny spider."

Beating rugs with metal rods, we shout a hymn as loudly as the girls in Tothill's chapel, our mouths wide, throats vibrating, chests heaving. Red-faced and gig-gling too.

Rock of ages, cleft for me.
Let me hide myself in thee!

Hannah calls us in to dinner. Soft bread dissolves in my mouth with a slice of kidney pie. Alice leaves half her portion of pie untouched. When she sees me staring at it, she nudges me to take it.

There's dessert too: egg custard, slippery sweet, slid-ing down my throat with hints of cinnamon.

"Mmm!" I hum.

"Orpha in ecstasy!" Sesina pipes up to a round of laughter.

"I've never tasted such...flavor!" I squeeze my eyes tight, almost blurting out the truth: I never ate egg cus-tard before.

Hannah applauds as Sesina and the girls laugh out loud.

I catch the girls' fire with my words, echoes of their laughs, and before they are quieted, spin them into more giggles again, with my oohs and aahs.

"Please tell me, when do we eat custard again?" I beg them.

·· ● ··

Mr. Dickens arrives today at the end of our spring-cleaning. My breath stops short whenever I think of what he will ask me next. I perch on a seesaw: *Will he keep me on? Will he let me go?* Up and down, back and forth I swing.

From the hallway, his voice now travels.

"Nothing on the chairs, Jemima. Tidy them at once. All knitting and books should be properly stored on the bottom shelves of the tables when not in use." Then, sniffing, he adds, "It smells clean here! Well done, girls. It's officially spring now."

Mr. Dickens finds me in the parlor, dusting books. The task has taken me hours, as I stand totally still, reading titles from all the spines.

"I wonder, Miss Wood"—he swipes his fingers along the shelf of a bookcase, eyeing it for dust—"if you might read to the other girls in the parlor tonight?"

My mouth falls open.

"Think of it as a way to let the other girls get to know you. They will be amazed. Besides, when Miss Macartney reads, have you noticed how they all doze off?" He smiles slyly.

"That book, sir, *The Whale*, is deadly. There's not one laugh in it. Boz's *Sketches* is funnier. Perhaps that's a better book to read to them?"

Mr. Dickens studies me. "You are free to read anything you like. But why that one? Indeed, why Boz?"

"It rings true, as if he walked London's streets beside us with its hackney stands and pawnbrokers. He makes great fun of it all."

Something happens in his eyes then: a glow.

As he leads me into the back parlor, I tell him more. "My pa said that in the rookery, *Sketches* was clutched like food. Nobody paid us any mind until Boz wrote of us. He made us cry, sir; he made us laugh."

His face rounds as if holding something inside, ready to burst.

"You must like to read him too, sir. Have you ever met him?"

His head is bowed to the black book. He motions me to sit.

"However can Boz write so true?"

Mr. Dickens raises his hands in the air. "Mostly he paces, watching everyone and everything. Thinking. Listening. Falling into such a spell that he sees no one in the room, for he must jot ideas down fast before he forgets them."

His words jump into the space between us. A rush like a thrill rises in my stomach. His hand scribbling before me at Tothill! Him pacing the floor unaware of the matron and me at the door!

"Have you guessed, Miss Wood?"

His eyes darken and land right on me as I gasp, "Boz!"

"I once was Boz, yes. I suppose I still am. It was a nickname I used when I first began to write. Until I had success. Then I wrote novels using my real name—the name you know me by now."

I am up on my feet, voice rising. "*You* can't be Boz!"

"Why not?"

"You are Mr. Dickens!"

"*Charles* Dickens, to be exact."

Then he leans back in his chair and shuts his eyes. He recites a page from Boz's *Pickwick Papers*, the muscles in his face jumping as he flits from character to character. It's a performance. First it's Mr. Pickwick talking and then Sam Weller. How could I forget these men, whose very speeches my pa performed for his own audience?

"Bah humbug! Let's try another," he says now. " 'Marley was dead, to begin with. There is no doubt whatever about that.' Do you know it?"

He cocks his head and recites more. I plop down in my chair like a heavy weight. I certainly do know those lines. It's *A Christmas Carol* by Mr. Charles Dickens! I stare at him with my mouth open. Charles Dickens I'd heard of, of course. It's a name known all around London. But how could this man be *the* Charles Dickens, the most famous writer in all of England? And he insists he is Boz too!

"Tell me who you really are, please, sir!"

"I am both: Boz and Charles Dickens. Writing is my livelihood."

Then he turns his head away as if listening to something far off. He's gone somewhere. I've seen it before. Right in front of me, he disappears. His lips mumble as if he's having a conversation with someone invisible. Then, for long minutes, his pen scratches inside a notebook. When he finally looks up from its page, his eyes seem vast and earthy brown. I wonder where he's been.

"What is it you are writing, sir?"

He smooths his tousled hair with his palms. "You must think me a madman. Words have been flashing and I can scarcely catch up with them. At home, in the fly on the way over here, and just now, they swoop down like gnats and won't leave me be."

"What's it about, sir?"

"Hmm…" He leans forward to study me. "I'm writing like the devil to finish the last month's serial of *Little Dorrit*. It's about a needlewoman who might fall if she is not saved. Wherever I go, shopmen shout their bad advice about a happy ending! They've never forgiven me Nell's death in *The Old Curiosity Shop*. I have to steer into alleyways to be rid of them!"

Mrs. Marchmont taps at the door to remind Mr. Dickens of his appointment with a workman soon.

"Let me know the instant he arrives." He raises his voice.

Then he turns abruptly to me. "Miss Wood, I trust you will keep my identity secret from the other girls?"

I swallow hard and nod.

"Good. Then let's continue with the interview. Since I have shared my secret name with you, it is only fair that you share your secrets with me. So let's start where we left off, shall we... at the workhouse?"

Bitter, bitter as a mouthful of lemons shoved down my throat when he says that. The others all confessed. I am next. The thick maroon book is wide open. *Case Book*, he has named it. And that quill never leaves his fingers.

"How did you come to leave the workhouse?"

"Aunt Agatha fetched me, along with her husband, back to the rookery. I turned cartwheels all the way to their rooms on Great St. Anne's Lane."

"What happened then?"

"My aunt said I must work with her."

"At what?"

"On the dust mounds by the Thames, sir. She was a feeder of dust and I was her sifter. Of bones and cinder. Of rags and charred coal bits. Of tin and oyster shells. Each piece weighed and sold to the street man for making soap, glue, soil, brick, and dye."

"This is how your family made their living?"

"During that time, my uncle's work became risky and my aunt went with him on the lookout. So she left me in the dust piles, sinking in dust and bones up to my chest. More than once, I had to be yanked out. The rot from bones brewing was awful. It could set you to coughing for weeks. Boys were quick to snatch from my pile. Those days, I went home to switchings."

"How long did you do that work?"

"Over a year."

"Was it such treatment that made you leave your family?"

I shake my head.

"Had you met someone?" he asks. "A boy from the theater, perhaps?"

I am mute. He sits and waits, a silent cat watching a mouse tiptoe out of its hole.

The words sneak out between the tight cords around my mouth. "I was...with child...and my aunt ordered me to leave at once."

My first thought back then was to run to the only friend I had: Emma, whom I had not seen since Pa died. But my belly spoke too loudly. No one would want to know a girl like that. I thought Emma had forgotten me, anyway. Not until the letter did I realize she was looking for me.

In Mr. Dickens's presence, my body turns to stone and I cannot budge it. It is used to doing that.

"Where did you go?" he demands. "You were only fourteen. Did you try to get help or ask your...lover for shelter?"

Ivy had a lover and Hester swore she had too many to count, having begun at twelve. It's all Sesina speaks of. Fanny had a lineup of men but they were customers, not lovers, like the soldier she whispers about. I cannot tell Mr. Dickens whose arms I slept in then. And they will not tell either. For they were dead. Between the stones in the graveyard was a safer place to sleep than the streets. After that, I was lost for good.

DICKENS'S CASE BOOK: NUMBER 98

Orpha has lived in all kinds of prisons. Forced into prostitution, young and alone, she was preyed upon. She does not seem at all coarse. Silent and reserved, she measures each word and notices everything, a street soldier on guard.

She says nothing to defend herself. It's almost as if she had nothing to do with becoming pregnant. Urania's girls all admit if they are virgins or not without batting an eye.

CD

Soon as Mr. Dickens has left, I rush straight to the parlor to examine the shelves until I find his true name: *Charles Dickens*. It dots the spines of books and monthly serials too. Two whole shelves of them! Ones by Boz too! I pull out the first one-shilling serial of *Little Dorrit* for myself. Then I pick a novel to read aloud, one by Charles Dickens.

As I turn to leave, I trip over something unseen and fly across the room, slamming into an oak desk. Behind me is a faint sound like skirts rustling. This is the day and hour Jemima dusts the parlor but she's nowhere to be seen.

·· ● ··

That evening, we gather in the parlor for needlework and literature. Miss Jane settles into her chair gracefully, propping her foot on a stool. After she introduces me as tonight's reader, Jemima mutters, "Isn't she the princess now?"

Deliberately, I turn away from her to announce the new book, *Oliver Twist*.

"Who the hell is he?" asks Jemima, hissing *hell*.

Miss Jane interjects in the same even tone she always uses, smothering Jemima's curse. "It's sure to be a delightful story if Orpha chooses to read it to us."

I begin. Needles click. Upon the mention of *workhouse* in the fourth line, one head rises. Next I read about the newborn Oliver, who struggles to breathe, the old drunken woman who is supposed to be helping, and finally the mother who asks to hold her baby before she dies. There I pause to look up.

All the girls' eyes are upon me, even Jemima's. Alice has dropped her needlepoint onto her lap and is wiping her eyes. She pulls so hard on her lungs, her chest squeaks. Sesina sits bolt upright, her mouth fallen open.

If only Ivy could be among us, her warm eyes signaling how she felt. All the ways she let me read her so that at any time, I could look at her and never feel alone.

"For God's sake, Orpha!" Jemima shouts. "Don't keep us all guessing. Read some more!"

I lower my eyes and read another chapter until it's time for prayer. By then, the boy is in deep trouble. Mr. Dickens is right: the girls are amazed. And so am I. None of them have any idea who Charles Dickens really is.

·· ● ··

Today, Mrs. Marchmont insists I walk out with the others. She hands me my shawl and hooks her arm firmly in mine so I cannot beg off. Outside, her hold on my arm does not budge. It's the first time I am wearing my sky-blue dress. It spreads wide at the hips, swaying with each step, giving my flat body curves. I imagine crowds, hands over their mouths, gossiping: *She's no virgin!*

On the road to market, we meet two women who

nod and walk past without staring. The village has one store that sells everything you need. Our bags soon fill with buttons, yarn, muslin, thread, and bright ribbon. The matron treats us to sweets, which we chomp immediately. Licorice blackens my mouth with fumes of anise. On the way back, Fanny hops. Leah slips her hand into mine and pulls me along, the three of us skipping in time. We seem like sisters. No one would ever guess what we really are.

·· ● ··

On Saturday afternoon, our benefactor, Miss Coutts, visits and everything around her fades. She's dressed in burgundy from her silk hat and veil down to her heeled boots. Folding her veil back, the lady motions me to sit across from her as she sips from her teacup like a hummingbird. Bergamot perfumes the room.

"Cat got your tongue?" Jemima whispers in my ear as she bends down to offer us oatcakes. She smiles sweetly at Miss Coutts as if she had a mouthful of sugar.

Miss Coutts removes her gloves. To see her hands could make one weep. Her skin is smooth and lily white, nails filed to ovals, all her long fingers dotted with rings. I sit on top of my own hands, still darkened with oakum.

"Mr. Dickens tells me you read novels. That is quite pleasing to hear. What do you enjoy so far about living at Urania?"

Her lips lift woodenly at the corners, almost as if she is too shy to smile. She's not like the male trustees: loud, all business, orders, and talk.

"Everything is alive here, miss. The girls chatting. Turning the earth for a garden. Richard the rooster struts as if he owns all the hens and the yard too. He'd never believe it's Urania who owns him!"

"Well put, Miss Wood." She smiles now. "You paint a picture of how simple, everyday things have their own beauty. And humor too."

"For two years, all I had was walls, miss."

"I am glad you wished to come to Urania. Are you?"

"It seems like I'm in a dream from which, any day now, I will awaken and be back at Tothill."

"Don't say that name!" Miss Coutts presses a finger over her lips. "You must never tell anyone you were there. Promise me!"

She fixes me with dark eyes and sits most erect.

I nod vigorously. How could I dare do anything else?

She lifts her cup of milky Indian tea and so do I. Never once did I imagine I'd be sitting with a lady from Piccadilly at teatime.

"Mr. Dickens has such praise for your voice. It's trained, he says. I'd like to hear you recite. In our next meeting...will you read to me?"

My face heats as I nod.

"By the time you leave here, you will be a first-class servant," she tells me. "Those who look upon you will only see a fine background and a sound education. And some finishing as well—"

She hands me a small leather case of grooming utensils. There is a bristle brush, which she instructs me to use morning and evening to keep my hair clean and free of oil. Rosemary water to wash my hair with monthly. A jar of cocoa-nut oil to smooth stray ends into a bun when my hair grows out. And a tiny file to trim my nails. Such things are meant to tame girls like me.

·· ● ··

Later Sesina says, "We didn't want to tell you about it. I'd spoil the surprise. But isn't it special?"

Never had I thought to groom myself other than with a splash of water for my stand-up wash. As I brush my hair in front of the mirror that night, counting the hundred strokes Sesina says I must make, I examine myself. A quiet girl from the rookery, only her eyes giving her away. They dart and darken, watchful. Pa used to call my hair silken wheat and blond. "You will draw them in, golden girl," he predicted. But that girl has gone.

Now my hair has browned. The crisp blue dress speaks of another girl, the one Mr. Dickens and Miss Coutts wish me to be: a first-class servant once I pass all their tests. I once dared believe I'd be something other.

· ● ● ·

One evening, Mrs. Marchmont leads a discussion in the parlor.

"We believe it's important for you girls to imagine your new lives once you leave England."

Fanny nods. "You won't catch me going back to the streets, I swear! Once I sail out of this country, I'll make good."

The matron nods. "What do you expect to find in the colonies?"

"Enough money," Leah responds. "A good position. A place to live."

"Decent work," Fanny says. "Where I don't have to sell myself."

"That is all behind you," the matron insists. "Miss Coutts has found placements for our senior girls, Alice and Hannah, who will emigrate together to Australia. Hannah will cook for a clergyman's family, and Alice will be the town's dressmaker—"

Sesina interrupts. "Miss Coutts mentioned marriage too?"

The matron nods. "Eligible farmers and miners will be reviewed by our contacts in the colonies. If you wish, you can marry someone suitable."

"What if he's ugly?" Fanny protests to a round of giggles.

"Beggars can't be choosers!" Jemima yells to more laughter.

"Girls!" The matron's voice rises. "It is up to you whom you pick. As married women, you will have security and a place in society."

From the top of the mantel, Rhena's photograph looks down on us. Big-bosomed and unsmiling, she emigrated to Canada a while ago. They say she has already married.

"What does Mr. Dickens think of us marrying?" Hannah wonders.

Our matron smiles widely at that and pulls a letter from her bag.

"I'll read from a letter he wrote to Miss Coutts about Urania when they were planning to open it… 'If even one woman goes on to a new life, with both work and marriage, think how far we can reach into the future. For their children will know a different life and have a better chance.'"

"Never imagined having my own children," Jemima mumbles. "Between no money and the gin, my parents couldn't care for me. But if I got a good man overseas, I'd start a family. Girls. No boys!"

Fanny sighs. "I always dreamed of having babies."

I keep my gaze down at my crocheting. No one must guess why I don't chime in. No one must know what happened.

I had a baby once and cannot tell where it is now.
I had wished a terrible thing: I wished it gone.

But not before I cursed myself dead first so Luther would never find me.

Ever since the arrest, accusations have screamed in my head: *Did I wrap the cord in my own bloodied hands and tie it around the baby's neck? Did I tug it hard before anyone saw it take a breath?*

·· ● ··

For hours after our discussion, even when we go upstairs to bed, all the girls gossip about is the colonies, their eyes glazing over as if they've been offered a whole gingerbread house to eat. Chatter about kangaroos and koalas buzzes throughout the hallway.

Transportation puzzles me. Why would anyone wish to leave England forever? I shudder to think of being booted to a far-off country where I'll know no one and from which I may never return. Yet I signed my name for Urania and gave it no more thought. I had to get away from Luther, didn't I? Mostly, I don't think of a future at all. It's only the past that seems alive.

·· ● ··

Tucked safe in my bed at night, I snuggle with *Little Dorrit*. The seamstress Dorrit is a soft presence floating through the book.

"Got a dirty book you're hiding underneath the covers?" Sesina calls over. "For we hear you gasping!"

I ignore her and return to my book. Dorrit is invisible, not wishing to be seen. Yet her stitches are so fine, her work is in demand. Though she sews for the upper class, as quiet as a mouse in a corner of their parlor, she can barely afford supper for her own family in the workhouse. That's what made me gasp. It's as if he scratched the Little Mouse right onto the page.

I love the nicknames. I want one too. The girls gossip about who is who and how she got that name. Cleanliness earned Hannah her nickname: Hedgehog. Everyone knows Jemima is Sticky Fingers because she stole. But what is it he secretly calls *me*?

Could he have his favorite? I don't. Hannah and Fanny confide in me; they don't speak out of the sides of their mouths like Sesina. Odd how in prison, a girl's nod or stolen glance spoke for her. Separate and silent, yet we were one.

The one precious thing in prison was Ivy. She always needed to know how I fared. Not a step or handshake could she make on her own. Just that penetrating look she dared and those secret hand signals passing between us in a language she invented. She held up a bright mirror for me to look into, keeping me alive.

Yet I haven't dared write her. Any letter will be read aloud by the matrons. But if I don't send word soon, Ivy will disappear and I might never see her again.

The last time I saw her, her fingers rattled the eyelet hard, her cries echoing my name through Tothill's frigid hallways. It's hard to think of her still kept there. Has she rebelled, only to prolong her stay? Or has Tothill smothered her in stone?

The very next day I write the simplest of words so she can read them herself:

Dear Ivy, Urania is a true home. You will be safe here with me. Please come!

Orpha

Mrs. Marchmont posts it that afternoon.

·· ● ··

During a lesson with the matron, I try to tame my yarn with a King Charles brocade pattern to make a Sunday shawl, counting stitches so the rows line up. Not one mistake can a girl make or it will show. After a month of knitting, I've guessed the places where one's mind can stretch, along the purl rows that slip by as simple and blind as oakum. Working those rows, I scarcely breathe; I scarcely am. My mind flattens.

I am visited by an image of that sparkling twilight dress falling to my feet. The one with the stars. It was my mother's dress, which I first wore at the theater one night while the next scene was being set up. When I looked at myself in the mirror, I discovered someone else beneath the costume. No longer was I eleven-year-old Orpha, but another being: Ophelia. She spoke through me as if I were a hollow reed. I had no other want but to please her sharp need to speak. When the actors shoved me before the loud and drunken audience, a bouquet of flowers in my hands, I chanted Ophelia's sad speech about Hamlet's mind so overthrown. The crowd was silent throughout, startled to hear a child who had memorized all those lines, roaring its pleasure at the end. Afterward, Pa greeted me with wide-open arms, although he could barely stand straight by that time of night. I was a girl with promise once.

Where do memories go after they brush through you? What if you wish to hold on to them forever?

I wonder if that is why Mr. Dickens writes.

·· ● ··

Some days later, when the afternoon mail arrives, we hear Miss Jane call.

"There's a letter for you, Leah! From London!"

"Oh!" Leah rushes into the parlor, pleading with Miss Jane to read it aloud.

"Your mum's taken a turn for the worse. She asks for you to come home now."

Miss Jane steadies Leah into a chair, patting her shoulder. "There, there, we'll see what we can do. The trustees are in a meeting right now. I'll let the matron know as soon as I can."

At supper, Leah just stares at the floor. She never takes a bite.

That evening, Mr. Dickens writes in the back parlor, then finally calls for Leah. When at last she comes out, she looks pale.

"He's sending me on the first omnibus to London tomorrow. It will bring Mum comfort to see me!"

Later, in our room, as we help pack her bag, she talks in a low monotone as if it hurts to even drop the words from her mouth.

"How many times did I beg her to run away from my father! She wouldn't do it. He beat her and drank up what little she earned selling flowers. Day after day of standing out in the streets in all kinds of weather...her consumption never healed."

Sesina wraps Leah in a hug. "I never knew my own mother. But you've told me so much of yours, I've loved her too."

"She's been my truest friend. And I hers. That was the one thing my father couldn't destroy. The hulks have him now if he hasn't shipped far off already. He finally got caught red-handed with somebody's silver. Thank God we will never see him again!"

That night, Leah sits straight up in bed with her eyes shut and lips mumbling every time I look over. I wonder if she is praying. At any time, something can happen to change your life forever. Afterward, you are never the same girl again.

·· ● ··

Come Friday the next week, there's persistent knocking at the front door. Only the matrons are allowed to answer, but neither one of them is around. Just Hannah, who nods for me to go because her hands are dripping in beef fat. I run to open it. And gasp.

A delivery boy stands there, his cap at a jaunty angle, legs spread wide, collar wide open, revealing his flushed, bare throat. Bloodstains dot the front of his shirt. Such a piercing gaze he has, bold as a crow. That's what he would be were he an animal. Which I think he is.

He piles parcels of freshly butchered meat into my arms. "Here's Urania's order. And tell Sesina Reuben called."

He stares knowingly at my chest like he can see the place where my breasts hide. Sharp and slicing, his eyes roam up and down. As if he knows the secrets I keep and guesses I am no virgin. It makes the bile rise up to my throat.

I slam the door in his face. And vow to never tell Sesina.

·· ● ··

We quietly embroider one afternoon. There's been no news of Leah since she left last week. While the matron gives sewing lessons, Alice busily sews the moiré fabric into curtains for the dining room. In the sunlit parlor, it shimmers a rich emerald green.

Suddenly Fanny stands up and cries out, "Mrs. Marchmont! I can't stay with Jemima one more second!

She calls me terrible names. And curses me too! I want another roommate."

"Well..." The matron takes a deep breath. "If someone volunteers to take your place, we can arrange it."

All eyes drop to their work.

Jemima flings her sewing project hard at Fanny's head. "You're just jealous. I'm what you can never be. A survivor! You're some soldier's leftovers. That's why you crawled into Magdalen Hospital with those prostitutes! And ended up at Coldbath!"

Before we can gasp, Fanny flies across the chairs and clutches Jemima's hair in her fists. Then Jemima kicks Fanny so hard in the shins that she tumbles.

Sesina claps as if at a play. "Collie shangles! Let her have it, Fanny! Give her a good batty-fang!"

Hannah, a square block of a girl, storms out of her seat and drags Fanny away from Jemima.

"That girl could hold a candle to the devil!" Hannah mutters, leading Fanny out of the room.

The matron plants her feet right in front of Jemima, hands on her hips. "We do not allow any fighting here. Go to your room right now. And stay there. Fanny will sleep downstairs tonight."

Jemima huffs up the stairs, kicking the banister as she goes.

"What shall we do now, ma'am?" Miss Jane squeezes her hands.

"I'd like to give that girl a good thrashing!" Mrs. Marchmont frowns. "But I shall do nothing of the sort. I have my instructions from Mr. Dickens. He must be informed immediately. I am under his orders to 'wait till I get there'! Until then, she stays in her room."

Zachariah is called to take a message to Mr. Dickens while Fanny rests in the kitchen. It is my turn to wash the evening dishes, so I join her there. It grows very late, after prayer. The girls head upstairs to bed. Just as I'm done, getting ready to follow them, Mr. Dickens storms in. His coat is unbuttoned, his hair uncombed.

"Jemima!" he yells in the hallway. "Come down here at once!"

Jemima appears in the top hall. Ever so slowly, she sulks down the steps.

I tiptoe back into the kitchen for one last check on Fanny, who slumps in a corner on a metal cot. Every muscle in her thin face has flattened. If only she would talk, it'd break the spell.

"Here, let me." I sit down beside her, unwinding her bun. "You mustn't mind her. Jemima's a bully."

Tears drop down her face. "She was right about me."

"No, she wasn't! She has a sharp tongue."

Fanny shakes her head. "I told her my secrets. I shouldn't have. And she twisted them into knots."

I stroke her hair as if she were a small child.

"A soldier I met at market kept begging me to sneak out with him. Said he was charmed by my beauty. Only for an hour, he said. I was barely thirteen. I stayed the night with him and lost my virginity. When I went home, my father refused to let me in. So I stayed on with the soldier."

She presses her forehead as if she has a headache.

"He disappeared with all my pocket money. I had no home to go to after. Only the streets. And leering customers. On account of him, I lost my family and all my decency. Why didn't my father tell me about keeping my virginity? Before I guessed what it was or how precious it could be, it was gone in one night!"

I rock Fanny back and forth, her head against my chest, until she falls asleep. Afterward, in the dark, tiptoeing upstairs, I curse how the night a man first touched you changed the direction of your whole life, both Fanny's and mine. I could have wept but did not.

DICKENS'S CASE BOOK

It is quite dark when I leave Urania. The matron protests, eager to call a fly to take me home. But she has read my face, all Thunder. My feet are on Fire and I must walk them out. My mind is scorched with images of these girls who were never children, Damaged from the start.

Jemima's anger threatens to dampen any chance of finding her a post. Another long talk with her tonight yielded nothing, her head turned away. "Feral," Chesterson aptly named her. She has one last chance here. How to defend her? How low Leah seemed on her way to London. Queen Bee Sesina stalks Urania, a motherless child who will always demand attention, mostly of the wrong sort. That devil-may-care attitude of hers is risky. Hannah, bruised by such violence that her life may never be normal. Fanny, making all the wrong choices. And Orpha, peeking out from behind Invisible bars.

In their lives, I see my own Shadows: a mother's Betrayal; my family's degradation in the Workhouse; my employment as a twelve-year-old at the blacking warehouse; my schooling abruptly ended. If I were female, I might have lived the same lives as these Homeless girls.

CD

·· NINE ··

In the cornfields, boys throw stones at crows gobbling seeds from the newly planted ground. Long past dusk, they chase after the thieves. On rainy days, the boys huddle, wrapped up in their own arms.

Out on the street, workmen dig gas lines. Urania will soon have its own gas jets instead of candlelight. Sesina and Fanny take turns peeking out the curtains at the men.

"Look how that dark-haired one stands, like he owns the whole street!" Sesina cries. "He's a genie from afar. I'll take him!"

Fanny protests. "I saw him first!"

Later that morning, Leah arrives, carpetbag in hand, dragging her feet. "My mum's bedridden. How long she has, nobody knows."

Hannah serves her tea in the parlor. Leah sips it quietly, staring out the window at nothing at all.

The postman delivers today's mail. Greedily, I sift through it, heart pounding. Nothing from Ivy. She should have received my note weeks ago. *Why doesn't she answer?* Instead, there's a letter with a strange stamp from faraway Canada, one of the colonies.

"Rhena hasn't forgotten us after all!" Sesina calls out.

"Give it here." Fanny snatches a daguerreotype of Rhena out of the envelope, a baby in her arms, beside a mustached husband.

She exclaims, "Look at the arms on that man! A lumberjack who works in the bush! And here's something else—a pencil sketch Rhena did of the log cabin he built for them."

At the sound of Mrs. Marchmont's voice, Fanny slips the papers back into the envelope and presents it to the matron.

"Good news from Rhena!" The matron reads aloud. " 'A son's been born to us, strong and healthy. Even with all the hard work in this Ontario wilderness, we are happy and prospering.' "

"Let me see!" Fanny peers over the matron's shoulder, pronouncing the syllables. "Lum-ber-jack! Look! I'm reading my first letter from a Urania girl. Ain't that something?"

"Someday soon, you'll be writing to us, Fanny." The matron smiles. "You'll be settled somewhere and have a family too."

Fanny leaps to her feet and twirls her skirts around.

"How Rhena's done it," Jemima mutters, "is anyone's guess."

"Quite a handful she was." Hannah smirks. "Came at

sixteen and ever so saucy. Dickens threatened to throw her out more than once, I heard. He'll be proud to read of her success now."

Mrs. Marchmont's lips turn down as she looks through the rest of the mail. Miss Jane leads her away, their muffled voices traveling from the kitchen. We girls speak of Polly and Agnes, gone to Australia, in whispers.

"They were due to arrive by now." Hannah pokes me. "We should have had a letter. Pray they arrived safe. The seas are fearsome!"

·· ● ··

In our darkened room, Sesina tosses. Leah has fallen deeply asleep.

"Will you tell me if I am a normal...girl, if I tell you a secret?"

Sheets rustle as Sesina sits up. *"Normal?"*

"If I bleed, does everything still work inside?"

"Girls are supposed to bleed. You *are* normal. I seen it."

"But can somebody take something out of you?"

"Who?"

"A doctor. A nurse. Those who condemn you. While you had fainted and don't remember?"

"Tell me what happened, Orpha. Then I'll tell you what I think."

It spills out like vomit. About the nurse in the hospital

saying, "We fixed it so you can't do business anymore and we ought to fix all girls like you." Sesina doesn't take her eyes off me.

At last she sighs. "So that's what happened! Bad enough luck to get pregnant but then be accused of even worse. I can't believe you were threatened by those who should have helped you!"

Have I heard anyone say those words? Never! My chest heaves.

Sesina says, "Don't worry, Orpha, you are on the mend. How many girls told me their bleeding stopped in prison. Those places make you feel dead. You *are* normal now. They didn't fix you. Can't be done!"

I don't want her to stop talking. Ever.

But I didn't tell her all. I could never tell all.

·· ● ··

The monthly committee calls me in the first week of May.

"Miss Wood." Dr. Brown addresses me. "We have been reviewing your case and discussing your progress here."

Oh, no! Haven't I steered clear of Jemima as the matron asked?

"Do you know why you were invited to Urania?" he asks.

A long pause. "So I can mend my ways and ... learn."

"Well, many critics believe that isn't possible." Dr. Brown sighs. "Some deem fallen girls 'irreclaimable,' meaning they will never fit into society again."

"Society be damned!" Mr. Dickens interrupts. "Urania teaches its girls skills so they can find work. That is what we do here."

"Mr. Dickens has spoken in your favor, Miss Wood." Dr. Brown suppresses a smile. "You exhibit a reserve most of our girls don't possess. And your literacy is remarkable, he insists. We feel that with your skills you will do very well as a governess."

All I can do is blink and hold my breath until I am dizzy.

"For God's sake, Brown, tell it in plain terms!" the governor says.

"Miss Wood, your trial period is over. You shall continue your education here until we find a position for you overseas."

Immediately I curtsy the way I was taught by Pa, lifting my long skirt, bending low, folding my chest deeply. The matron glows; she said nothing of Jemima after all. Her lips lift into a smile. She could have blown me over with a breath.

DICKENS'S CASE BOOK: NUMBER 98

She's an Actress through and through. Curtsies like she was born to it. Full of secret hiding places where she tucks things away. Sometimes I get a *glimpse of her but then she disappears right in front of you, submerged in a London pea soup fog.*

How like Ophelia she is! A tragic girl, Betrayed by all.

CD

I measure myself against Sesina. Shoulder to shoulder in front of the mirror, we each study the other one. She is taller, mysterious beneath her curly locks, while I am petite, pale, and brown-headed, with heavy, straight hair that hangs like a horse's mane.

"If you were properly groomed, you'd be an eyeful." Sesina shifts her eyes my way. "And the way you glide, light-footed as a willow branch. If only you'd smile!"

She slides her own hair clip to hold my bangs in place, then cinches my waist with a belt. Little wisps of my locks she trims now, teasing them to fall over my forehead.

"There! You look prettier now."

We turn back to the mirror. Sesina leans closer, turning my face to hers, then strokes my cheek with one long finger. She smiles as if she owns me.

·· • ··

The following week, Mr. Dickens suddenly rushes in late, breathless, from a speaking engagement, in a black velvet frock coat to which a gold watch is chained. A scarlet silk tie peeks out at his neck and a glimpse of stripes flashes beneath his coat.

He's come for my confession. Once he hears it, he will not keep me here.

"You are always writing, sir." I point to his thick book, so full of unmentionable secrets that it must be locked up each and every night.

"True—in this Case Book. But I also bring along my own notebook to jot down 'mems'—little notes and ideas to further my novels. On the way home from here, a whole scene can take shape in my head and write itself from those few words."

"How did you become a writer?"

"My father was a great storyteller. Some would even say a fabricator." He laughs. "And I was early a listener, often sickly, and a reader too. Words hold a charge. The right words are alchemy."

"I saw alchemy in a play once. Magicians turned metal into gold. But can words change anything, sir?"

I wonder who would ever listen to words from a prostitute, for that is what I am called, even by Mr. Dickens. *There are worse secrets only I know of, forbidden acts, that society would shudder to know. But such stories won't ever be told. Not by him. Not by me.*

"London is changing. When readers meet a child

laborer in my pages, they petition Parliament to open schools. Indeed, Miss Coutts began Urania because of the desperate women I wrote of."

"You seem possessed by words, sir."

Mr. Dickens stares at me. "I've always lived in my books, stepped inside and completely disappeared. I had to."

It's me who needed to hide, not him. Why would such a famous man need to do that?

"I made up other worlds...when I was young. My family"—he pauses, looking into the distance—"betrayed me. No need to say how or why. I could not change what happened, but I could float to another world. I've gone there ever since."

"When I read a good book, sir, I enter another room and disappear from this one." I lean toward him. "Words are alive, sir! They carry what one thinks and feels to the world."

He gasps. "Why, that's exactly how words feel to me."

"All the words in the world were stored in my father's head. Rhymes. Speeches. Song. I learned to memorize them just as he did. He was a storyteller just like your own father."

"Hmm...your father must have been quite a character."

I edge forward in my seat. The long, wiry beard and untamed ends of his hair come into view, then his bushy eyebrows and, beneath them, the darkening fire of his eyes.

"But what do you do, sir, when words make pictures, like plays acting out in your mind?"

His eyes change then, brightening from dark to blue. "I know the problem well. You've seen my shorthand before—"

Suddenly I recall him writing at the prison desk. "Those strange squiggles, sir? Like chicken tracks in the dirt. Nobody can read them!"

He leans his head back and roars in laughter. "Long ago as a reporter, I trained myself to jot notes quickly to keep pace with my thoughts. But...you only need take quick notes to begin with. Words. Phrases. A sentence or two. Later, you can build a story on the skeleton of those few jottings."

He puts his quill down then. Not one awful note has he written in the Case Book today. He studies me for long minutes until it seems we both breathe the same breath. Our bodies are sitting there in the room, but we are not. There's a rap at the door and Miss Jane's voice announces that the governor is here to speak to him. Reluctantly, I rise to leave.

DICKENS'S CASE BOOK: NUMBER 98

I must take another track with this girl. I believe she will yield her secrets once she is ready. Insisting will only freeze her. First, she must trust me totally. That shall be my task now.

She charms me away from my task, guessing my real weakness: Writing is my first and, perhaps, only love.

CD

I have had my eye on Richard the Third, that cocky red combed rooster, crowing at all times of day. Sneaking up behind him, I grab him, squawking in my hands like I was a murderess, and pluck the longest white feather from his tail. I have my prize quill.

It must be sharp like a weapon. So I slide the sleek paring knife from where it's been tucked in my boot and whittle the shaft to a keen point. Dirt mixed with rainwater from a barrel is next. This I stir into a paste inside a rusty tea tin. It will do for ink.

In the chicken coop, behind a wallboard, I've hidden yellowed newsprint along with Emma's letter. No one will know what I am doing out here. It is my own private office, where no girl will pry. Outside, the hens cluck. They will be my guards in case anyone comes...

Images pulse. I'm seeing her. The rooster's quill begins to scrape.

Ivy speaks to me from her dark cell, her button-brown eyes upon me. How tiny she is, a speck in a high prison. I imagine what she'd say if there were no walls and no miles between us: *I'm breaking into chips, crumbling into dust. A hollow girl. He's gone! You're gone! There's no one left who knows me anymore.*

•• • ••

From the third-floor window, Reuben's cap appears at the top of the fence after Zachariah leaves on an errand. Sesina leans on tiptoe against the inner side of the fence, balanced on crates. She reaches up to Reuben as he hangs over to touch her hand. He tucks something into her open palms: a bottle shimmering like clear liquid in the sun. Gin! Sesina shoves it down her bodice and grins. He has a huge mouth and looks ready to gobble her. In the next moment, he's gone.

•• • ••

Tiny seeds have been tucked into my garden plot. There will be rows of beans, spinach, onions, and carrots beside the chives.

"Such perfectly straight rows you have hoed! In the colonies, you will have your own allotment." Mrs. Marchmont steps outside to inspect my task. "There you can be self-sufficient, feeding yourself and others with very little money. Even the Queen and Prince Albert's children tend gardens."

"Doesn't he have nine children?" I gasp. "And besides, he's rich!"

"He believes, as do many of us," she says, smiling, "that tending a garden develops gentleness in one's nature."

"Well, I can't wait to eat lettuce in three weeks' time!"

The matron sits down on a bench, the first time I've seen her rest in the middle of the day. "My own children tended a garden, running into the kitchen with handfuls of freshly picked vegetables, so excited!"

She's never spoken of her own life before Urania. Mother. Widow. Tothill matron. All kinds of girls must have tried her patience at Urania. Yet she often smiles and pats my shoulder after a chore well done, as one does with a child.

"Do you miss your family?"

She looks up and nods. "Very much. We write to each other often. My children are grown and on their own now. They've made me proud."

"You are still raising children here." I smile. "And it is certain that you know how to do so."

She smacks her hands on the bench as if I've told a joke, startling the chickens, setting them clucking.

"It's all I know how to do!" She laughs.

To finish my chore, I tuck only ten lettuce seeds into the cool soil, as Hannah advises, saving the rest for the weeks to come so there will always be young lettuce growing. Nearby, brown clematis stems climb. High up on their tops, tiny green leaves sprout. As I wish to do.

·· ● ··

Today the first blade of spinach spreads three emerald arms wide and waves in the spring wind. Seeds have their future locked inside them. What they will be, they already are. If they are given light, soil, and water, it almost happens all by itself.

In our chicken broth that evening, my flat, oniony chives are chopped into the soft dumplings, greening our mouths.

·· ● ··

Some days later, Leah drags herself upstairs and plops onto her bed, groaning. She has just changed rags that bled through her underclothes earlier.

"At least you know you aren't pregnant if you bleed," Sesina tells her.

Leah blushes. "Don't!"

Sesina's eyes narrow. "I won't. But our roommate had a baby. Didn't you know?"

Leah's mouth drops. My own breath stops. *The hand, the hand was over my mouth.*

Complete silence fills the room afterward; then the smoky snuffing out of candles. Sesina drifts off to sleep. Leah sits up in bed. She makes a hissing sound and points to the door. I follow her out.

"So that's what she's been hinting at about you," she whispers, looking around in the dark. "Best I tell you myself before she does. I came close to getting pregnant. Didn't guess such a thing could happen. What saved me was I was too young: I was ten."

My whole body stiffens. She was just a child.

That's what Luther did.

A door creaks open down the hallway.

"Are you girls still up?" Miss Jane calls. "Go back to bed."

·· ● ··

Rushing into the house the following Saturday with an armload of lemon balm for tea, I find Miss Coutts already waiting, dressed in soft mauve, like a lilac in bloom.

"Let me take that." Miss Jane opens her hands. She already has the copper kettle on the boil. "You tidy up first."

I return in fresh clothing, hair tucked back with clips into a tidy bun. There was no time to scrub my nails. Miss Coutts hands me a tiny bottle as a gift. As I open it, a floral scent fills the room, sweet and light. Lavender lotion! Tears spring to my eyes.

She leans toward me. "Oh! I am so sorry. What is the matter?"

Her long, slender fingers touching mine, risking the matron's eye. A flicker of her pressing into me, vanishing in a moment.

"It's just…a…memory of a friend. One as kind as you."

"That is what I hope to be for you too, Orpha: a friend; a confidante. Tell me about her."

She reaches across, tipping the open bottle into my palms, spilling its flowery scent.

"I thought Ivy would be my true friend, just like my childhood friend, Emma. But I'm not certain I'll ever see either of them again. Ivy hasn't answered my letter at Tothill. Perhaps I'm to blame. For I never answered Emma's letter either."

"Your friend Emma has written you?"

"Yes. At Tothill."

The letter, folded and refolded so many times, is falling apart now. It's harder and harder to read her words: *Tell me the truth and I will come.*

"Perhaps, when you are ready, you will write to Emma. It takes time to heal from prison life. And all that came before. You must first let go of all your hardship, receive our guidance, and rebuild your life. That's why you are here."

"I've begged Ivy to come to Urania. She has no plans. Nowhere to go. No family. And with what's she learned from her Jack—"

"I'll see what I can do."

My benefactor jots in a slim notebook after hearing

more of the story about my friends: one at Tothill and the other in the rookery.

"Mr. Dickens says you founded Urania after reading his novels."

"It bothered me to read of girls so abused. The evidence was right in front of me. Girls roamed the streets of Piccadilly, sitting on my front steps, between customers. Girls of twelve, painted bright as parrots, all starving. It seemed someone must help them."

Our eyes meet above our teacups. A knowing look passes between us.

"I hope you know that I…I am not one of those girls walking the streets. Circumstances led me to fall."

She sits back to sip her tea, blushing. "I already knew that about you, Miss Wood. You don't have to tell me."

·· ● ··

The girls are all chattering excitedly after Miss Coutts leaves, lined up at the window, watching her step into a waiting carriage.

Leah sighs. "Her dress is so soft, it floats as she walks!"

"Must be silk," says Hannah. "Bet it's from Paris!"

Alice whispers, "Such a gauzy silk. So delicate. Could have been spun by spiders!"

"She's loaded with money, that one." Fanny laughs.

"And she spends it on us, imagine that! To run this house and send us to far-off places."

"I heard she lives in a mansion with a lady companion like a queen!" Hannah exclaims.

"She's not married," Jemima says. "Not tied down to any man."

Sesina pipes up. "That's why she can pay for Urania. If she was married, a man wouldn't let her. He'd want her money for himself."

She's more than all they say. Today, I saw a depth in the lady beyond the beauty of her dress. Today, I felt her heart reach out to mine.

·· ● ··

It's the middle of the month. The committee meeting is assembling. The men are arriving. The matron passes me on her way to them.

"All morning, you've been pacing back and forth in the hallway. What are you worried about, Orpha?"

I protest. "It's ever so easy with you and Miss Coutts. You are both used to being with us girls. But I can't tell those men anything."

"You're too quiet, my girl, always thinking. But you must learn to speak your mind too."

I take a deep breath and the troubles tumble out: Ivy, with nowhere to go; that stench following Rose wherever she walked.

"Have you any news of them?" I beg her.

"They may have been discussed in private, I don't really know. There's only one way to find out—ask!"

I shake my head.

"Then *I* will," she insists.

I can't speak up. She never lived as I did, back slammed to the wall, waiting for the chance to run.

·· • ··

Now I stand before them, boots freshly blackened. Governor Chesterson frowns, folding his arms across his belly. His glance shifts to the other men, then drills me down.

I edge my feet closer to where Mr. Dickens is sitting.

"Miss Wood is concerned about her friend Ivy at Tothill," the matron begins. "Has she applied yet to Urania?"

Mr. Dickens strokes his beard. "Yes, she has. Though she has more interest in godforsaken Tasmania than in Urania, yet she seems promising. Orpha is attached to her, I see. Friendship is essential for our girls to succeed in life."

"When will you know, sir?" The words pop out of me without thinking. "She's due to be released come summer and I—"

"Urania needs to have a free bed first," the big-voiced governor interrupts. "As of now, there is none. And we make our selections according to who is neediest and most promising. We have a long list of suitable girls."

Dr. Brown shoots him a glance.

"And Rose?" the matron continues. "Also at Tothill?"

Mr. Dickens clears his throat and does not look straight at me.

It's as if all the air in the room got sucked away.

Mr. Dickens's eyes darken as he turns to me. "We are working to release her early so she can go home to her mother very soon. Her phossy jaw is fatal, I'm sorry to say."

"Whatever has happened to the girl?" Reverend Illingworth asks.

"She worked in a matchstick factory breathing phosphorus fumes far too many years. The vapors ate away the flesh of her jaw and all its bones. Soon she won't be able to swallow food at all. Yet she sings hymns, they tell me, and her crime was so minimal, she would have been ideal for the Home."

Murmurs circle the room. Tears bathe my face. I beg leave to go, one hand to the wall to guide myself out, the other over my mouth. I dare not ask about Edwina after that.

·· ● ··

They think I am doing nothing except sitting on the garden bench for the free hour after dinner. Images flow:

Rose holding her jaw, alone in her damp cell. She was cast off like an old garment the factory decided was of no use, once she sickened. Yet, even in her pain, she sang about something called *grace*. It's what lifts someone up when they fall flat. Like wind to a stalled ship. Lines of Rose's hymn echo down Tothill's hallway and enter my cell:

Amazing grace, how sweet the sound. . . .
'Tis grace hath brought me safe thus far
And grace will lead me home!

I know what Mr. Dickens does when the fever of words and images overtakes him. I have seen him in such a frenzy many a time. He stabs the words down with his quill at once, listening so carefully that he turns blind, deaf, and dumb to the world around him.

Does it help the pain to lift, I wonder, if you write it down and set it apart from the rest of you?

··•··

Come home at once! the note delivered by the messenger instructs Leah a few days later. Miss Jane accompanies her to the omnibus, returning that evening, alone.

"We arrived just in time." Miss Jane wipes tears away. "Leah said her goodbyes before her mother passed."

"We'll let Mr. Dickens know," the matron tells her. "Leah will need time to attend to her mother's burial."

There is a hush at Urania all that day as if we walk in Leah's footsteps. Who wept for my mother besides me? Her death ended with my father and uncle drinking themselves into a stupor at my aunt's, me waiting at the window all that night like a lit candle, searching for Ma.

I remember Emma shadowing me after I lost my own mother, afraid to leave me alone. I have not forgotten. But she must think I have forgotten her by now. Later that afternoon, I pry the letter out of hiding, hold it tight to my heart, and let her read what is written there. I could never tell it face-to-face.

The decision is final. *She can't know the truth. Ever!*

The letter shreds when tucked into the slats again.

·· ● ··

Tonight, beneath the bright gaslight illuminating his face, Mr. Dickens eyes me expectantly.

"Have you spoken to Edwina about Urania, sir?"

Mr. Dickens takes a deep breath. "She is most eager to come. But I decided not to see her once I read her medical report."

"The limp, sir? If she lived in comfort here, with a soft bed—"

Mr. Dickens shakes his head. "She has a venereal disease, so advanced, it cannot be cured."

I rise from my chair. "She's not that kind of girl!"

"Edwina never realized she had syphilis until her episodes of pain at Tothill. Likely she had it all her life, born to a mother who carried the disease. The governor is allowing mercury and laudanum until her release."

Edwina shook her head when asked about her mother: "She left home when I was young. Back to the streets to work, my aunt said, where they knew her."

"If… Edwina came to Urania, I'd care for her!"

"There is no future for her here. Or anywhere. Her disease will likely kill her within a few years. Miss Coutts only accepts girls who will go on to lead productive lives in the colonies."

I plop down in my seat, cheeks burning. If he refuses to interview Edwina, why should he see a real criminal like Ivy? She's already applied, he said. Yet she never wrote to me. Whatever could have happened to her since? Both she and Edwina are waiting in their cells to hear from him, but no answer comes. Come summer, Ivy will be released to the streets. We all know what happens to girls like that.

DICKENS'S CASE BOOK: NUMBER 98

Fire burns in this girl now. She is utterly other than she was at Tothill.

It is helping her to confess in bits and to speak of the wretched. Tothill's girls have all been sorely used just as she has. She cries for them, but never for herself. Ophelia looms over her own past like a Crimean guard.

She does not live here altogether but inhabits subterranean places where she feels safe. Such a haven is deeply entrenched in Imagination. That realm can be either a cure or a curse. Don't I know it too?

Perhaps we plucked her just in time. She was about to Evaporate.

CD

Perfumed red peonies picked from Urania's garden greet Leah when she returns, her mother buried in a pauper's grave. Her eyes expand when she sees them. She's thinner and paler but stands straighter than she ever did.

"I am ready to leave England now." She turns to the window. "The sooner the better. This country has only brought me sorrow."

· · ● · ·

One night near the month's end, Mr. Dickens works until late. When he finally steps into the front parlor, Hannah serves him tea. He flops down with a groan into a chair and observes us over the rim of his teacup.

Fanny knits her shawl furiously, eyes never leaving the stitches. Her fingers flit so fast, nobody can catch the moves.

Mr. Dickens gasps. "Wherever did you learn to spar like that with those needles, Fanny? Did you spear fish for a living, perhaps? If you keep up that kind of race, you shall finish before bedtime!"

"Well, sir, I'm dropping all my problems down into my knitting. Each one with a name: Edward, the soldier who betrayed me; Morgan, my first customer; Jed, my pimp. Trapping them in this wool like bugs in a spider's web. Leave them danglin' as they did me."

Bobbles dot her dark green shawl, little round bumps with clumps of stitches piled together, all with men's names.

"What a curious idea!" Mr. Dickens strokes his beard. "To imprint those names into your knitting as a . . . a sort of record, would you say?"

"As revenge, sir. Hang 'em all!"

Mr. Dickens drops his head back and lets loose a belly laugh. Immediately, like claps in response to a performance, he is joined by rounds of our giggles. Every time we look at him, a proper gentleman wiping tears from his eyes, we are so shocked, we start laughing again.

Fanny hoots the loudest of all. Even Leah is forced to laugh. Afterward, having drained two more cups of tea, he pushes himself up with a sigh to take the long walk home in the rain.

"No fly this evening, Mrs. Marchmont!" He raises his palms flat.

His hand fumbles in his pocket. A notebook drops out, which he picks up, jotting something into it before hurrying out.

The matron shakes her head. "He's off on one of his 'benders' again. That's what he calls those night walks of his. The signs are there: staring all about like an animal in a cage; his hair every which way; not looking at you."

In her corner, Miss Jane sighs. "He says he wanders London's streets long past midnight trying to stamp down his restlessness. The man's a genius, but I worry for his sanity."

"His safety too," the matron adds.

·· ● ··

He did it again tonight. When an idea comes, he jots it down. Like Fanny, gathering revenge into her stitches. Are his words his own wounds he can reveal no other way? All that night, I lie unsleeping, with great shivers of wonder.

Is it possible for a fallen girl like me to leap out of her old life into the shelter of words?

I've walked the whole night, scheming about Urania. These girls are Calculating: Fanny's nimble fingers seeking revenge; Sesina's eyes darting out the window. Such Restlessness is a signal. Currents run through them all, wild and unpredictable, hurts unimaginable, never forgiven.

Can Urania ever tame them? Surely the presence of hearth and family should calm them. Yet it has not done so for me for some years now. Everything Wars inside me, threatening to burn itself out.

Urania's girls need to have the comfort of Home, the very thing they never had, so elusive, it threatens to slip through my own hands this very moment.

CD

"*Something* got you into Tothill, Orpha," Fanny teases one evening in the parlor. "Let me guess: trouble!"

"Bet it was a man!" Jemima calls over, eyes on her knitting.

"It's always a man, ain't it? I heard you had a baby too."

The sucking in of breath fills the room. All heads turn my way. Alice's mouth falls open. *They weren't supposed to know.* My glance lands smack on Sesina, who leans back in her chair, smirking.

Leah stutters. "We—we're...not...allowed to know one another's stories. Mr. Dickens says we must keep them private."

"Dickens gets our stories for free, don't he?" Jemima spits her words like gravel. "And what does he do with them?"

Hannah glares at her. "It's his job to know them."

"But he don't tell us his!" Sesina whines.

"His what?" demands Hannah.

Sesina bangs her hand on the table. "His *own* secrets!

He grabs ours like a child demanding a lollipop. Don't you wonder what he's doing with 'em?"

"I told Dickens about my sorrows," snaps Hannah. "My heart is lighter for it."

Alice's voice trails across the parlor. "What is it about that man that makes you want to tell him everything?"

"Well, I told my stories to Leah." Sesina lifts her chin like a weapon. "And she's told me hers. That's enough for me."

Leah suddenly stands up, her face flushing.

"You pried them out of me, and Orpha too! You know exactly how to steal our secrets!"

Leah rushes upstairs. Sesina stalks a few steps behind her.

All eyes now look my way. Jemima turns her head expectantly.

So they think they know all about me. Just because of a baby that was never mine. It was always his. But Mr. Dickens has shared something with me that the others won't ever know. His true identity is my secret.

I face Jemima. "Mr. Dickens has troubles, same as us. But he carries on, in spite of them. And so do I. My past is *my* business. I'd never share it with the likes of you."

Jemima argues. "He don't have the problems you and me do—money, men, a decent living, a home. He's got what he wants."

"Who would want to spend their evenings with the lot of us"—Fanny shrugs—"instead of dancing and drinking? It's unnatural."

Jemima sneers. "Sesina says he must be paid plenty to come here. Just look at his silk ties and those fancy outfits of his. What a dandy!"

I get up and walk away from them, passing the bookcases. Even from far off, I can pick out his novels sitting quietly upon those upper shelves without anyone knowing: *Bleak House. David Copperfield. Hard Times.*

Girls like us turn into his characters. We live in his imagination.

We are the stars of Urania, his unnamed muses.

·· ● ··

Mr. Dickens never speaks of his wife, though they say he has ten children, one starting school and the oldest in university. It's as if his family lives in a foreign country. He abandons them when he visits us, a few hours away by foot. All the while, his mind is so burdened by stories, they never let him be. He's in a race to tell the world everything.

Mr. Dickens studies us girls all the time, I catch him at it. He's copying us. That's why the characters in his novels fly into a reader's mind and cling there like ghosts. They once were somebody real; they once were alive like us.

My boots suddenly stop in the middle of pacing the parlor. Deep inside, ideas are breeding. By the time I slip inside the shed and aim my quill, words march across the page like black ants. A word written down brings Pa a step closer. Just like Ivy, bits and pieces of my father appear from far off. Writing is a way of remembering, of calling people back from the dark.

·· ● ··

Jemima stands in the darkened hallway, barring the door to my bedroom. Her hard voice hisses into my ears. "I saw how your face dropped soon as I said *baby*. Not all pigeon-eyed like Fanny about her man. You didn't love him, did you?"

Jemima slides so near, her hot breath blows against my neck.

"Did he force you? Bet that's it. If I was you, I'd get revenge instead of sitting around this shithole reading books." Then she sneers. "Track him down. Chiv him good. Deep in the belly!"

Shivers prickle my neck. *A stabbing!* If ever a man deserved that, it'd be him. In that moment, Luther's face appears like vapor. *He can no longer find me but I know exactly where he is: the very lane; the very house; the very tavern. I could find him at any time.*

I should shout for the matron. But no one must know what Jemima just said. I back away, holding on to the wall, to stop my hands from slamming her flat.

·· ● ··

On the sunny windowsill of our bedroom, a glass of water is set. Inside floats something pale and wormy.

"Ugh, what is *that*?" Leah whispers.

Sesina tosses her curls. "Take a guess."

Leah and I stare at the worm waving in the sunlight.

Suddenly Leah covers her mouth. "It's not...It can't be!"

Sesina throws her head back and laughs.

A blush colors Leah's cheeks. "Well, I never!"

"Never what? Saw one before? Or used one?" Sesina pipes up. "If you use them, you're safe. If you don't, watch out!"

"What is it?" I ask finally.

"Sheep gut." Sesina smirks. "Has to be soaked before you use it. I'm getting it ready right now, in case there's a chance."

"For you and Reuben?" Leah gasps.

Sesina puts her finger over her mouth. "Better not tell! Or I'll tell plenty about the likes of you two if you squeal."

"But—however did you get it?" I blurt out.

A little cat grin spreads over Sesina's face. "I have my ways. You can use it over and over. As long as it don't rip. I'll have to teach Reuben not to buck so hard. If I can!"

·· • ··

On the first reading of *Oliver Twist*, the girls were mute. Only if I dared pause did they protest. But now that they have taken Oliver's side, they won't be quiet. They constantly interrupt the reading.

"Blasted! Now a baby farm's got him!" Hannah shouts in the middle of a paragraph, halting me.

"What's he kept there for?" Leah wonders.

"Just you wait," Fanny mutters. "Worse is coming."

And so it is. It's hard to read how the starving Oliver fares in the workhouse at nine years old. The night's reading ends with Oliver begging for more food.

"Oh, why did he have to do that!" screams Jemima.

Alice frowns. "What will happen to the boy now?"

"They'll get rid of him." Fanny looks up from her knitting. "Mark my words."

The assistant matron clears her throat. "Girls, if the novel upsets you so, perhaps Orpha should not go on."

"Don't you dare stop reading!" Sesina stamps her foot. "We all love Oliver. And we can't help it if he seems real."

"Oliver's one of us!" cries Hannah.

Miss Jane turns away, biting her lips. Her eyes catch mine and then I have to hide my own smile. After the reading, while the girls head upstairs, she beckons me to stay.

"Oliver *is* like many of us. I know what it's like to live with part of you amiss."

Her words ring in the empty room. I become very still. It's not my place to ever ask about her life.

She continues. "I was set apart by my limp. Unlike other young girls, I was not considered marriageable."

"But...you are so accomplished. Indeed, you are pretty too."

"I took every opportunity to educate myself: keeping records for my father's cloth importing business and ordering his supplies. At first, he wouldn't let me. Then, bit by bit, he allowed it. He knew I would have to support myself without the help of any man. And so I have."

She surprises me by telling me her age: twenty-one! Not much older than us.

"You have so many skills, Miss Jane. How I wish I could do the same as you."

"You already do!" She smiles shyly. "You're a clever girl. An actress. Trained by your father, as I have been. I've seen how closely you listen to everyone, including Mr. Dickens. That's how one learns. And I must confess to having seen you carrying a quill too. Are you writing?"

"I am trying to."

"That's a very good practice. It must make you feel better to tell your story. Even if it's only to yourself."

That's the very thing I cannot do. Ever. For no one must know.

"If you ever need...to talk or...want to share your writing, I'll give a listen," she says before bidding me good night.

Tell me again—I wish to pull her back by her sleeve—*that it's possible a girl like me can go on, in spite of everything. Tell me again.*

·· ● ··

The next afternoon, Miss Jane calls from downstairs. "Wherever has Sesina gone? She's late for cooking soup. Is she up there with you?"

From high on the landing, I shake my head. Leah, standing beside the assistant matron, stutters, "Oh, I... I...I just saw her pass by! Let me go look for her."

On the windowsill of our room, the glass sits empty. Later that afternoon, Sesina steals in, slinking up the stairs, on silent toes.

·· ● ··

From across the parlor that evening, Sesina yawns loudly, stretching her back like a cat after its nap. Fanny drills her eyes on her, knitting without once glancing down at her stitches.

"Damn it!" Fanny complains. "Now I have to yank out three whole rows. It's all messed. I forgot to purl the first row."

Sesina spins around to watch Miss Jane, whose head is bent as she examines Leah's needlepoint. She does not look up. Sesina lifts her chin high and smirks at Fanny.

On the settee, I sit beside Alice for a needlepoint lesson as she demonstrates how to use a thimble to protect my fingers from the needle's sharp jab. A coughing fit suddenly overcomes her. Her breath sounds like wind scraping through tunnels. She seems as fragile as a stitch.

"Here's the formula," she instructs, catching her breath. "Needle held ready. Needle to the work. Take up the stitch. Push with the thimble. Take hold of the needle and pull it through."

Alice watches as I work the needle with the thimble. "Hold the work steady, Orpha. The fabric must be stretched so the hard needle slides in easy, all the way through."

Jemima elbows Fanny. "You hear those instructions? Bet you can do that real easy!"

There is the sound of a slap. This time, Miss Jane immediately raises her head. Fanny jumps up, crosses the room, and plops down on the opposite side of the parlor. All eyes swing to Jemima.

"What?" She grins. "I was just saying how Fanny sews so fine, that's all. Can't a girl take a compliment?"

Miss Jane's eyes narrow. There's something gentle about her. Or is it genteel? She doesn't wring chickens' necks like our matron. Yet she's always watching and waiting, ready to say what's needed. She never raises her voice to scold, even when she should. I wonder what she tells the matron about us.

Alice bows her head, lost in her sewing, fingers running like a stream through the fabric draped over her. She barely finishes half her plate while the rest of us fight to grab her leftovers. What has stilled her and keeps her there, unlike the rest of us, growing bolder by the day?

·· ● ··

Back in our own room, Sesina hums to herself at the bureau, where she tucks the shrunken sheep gut into an empty chocolate box, powdering it with talcum.

"Worth the threepence he paid!" She sighs. "I'd pay any price for it!"

"Weren't you worried they'd catch you?" Leah gasps.

Sesina hoots. "Who—me? The only time I ever fret is when I don't get what I want!"

How like a raven she is, calculating its prey. I know where she went—the chicken shed. God only knows how I've hidden there too.

·· ● ··

I read aloud a description of Dorrit, the troubled needle-woman in *Little Dorrit*, to Miss Coutts. At the dramatic moments in the novel, I lift my chin and open my throat wide, throwing my voice across the whole room.

"How beautifully you present the scene, Orpha! Mr. Dickens is right—what a fine voice you have! I feel as if I'm attending a play. Your tone reflects deep sympathy for women mistreated by society."

"Miss, the rookery was filled with girls like Dorrit. Prison too."

"Our society punishes at once without recognizing that suffering is the real problem. My family befriended Mr. Dickens after reading his *Oliver Twist*. That novel about children in workhouses and street gangs preying on orphaned children so disturbed my father that he investigated immediately to see if it was true. It was indeed."

"Is this how you became interested in charity?"

"As a member of Parliament, my father petitioned to improve conditions at Coldbath Prison. What he found there so horrified him that he rallied for the oppressed. So Mr. Dickens speaks directly to my own family when he writes of social injustice."

She sips her tea, then leans closer to me. "Our Mr. Dickens told me how surprised you were to discover he is the author of this novel and many others."

She continues. "Can you promise me something? Don't tell the others. It might confuse them. Certainly it will distract them to know how famous our Mr. Dickens is. Our girls look to him as a father. Don't you agree?"

"I've already told Mr. Dickens I'd keep his secret. None of the girls have come close to a guess, miss. They don't know his books! I would never give him away. Some do see him as a father. Hannah does."

"And you, my dear—how do you view him now that you know who he really is?"

A long pause. "Much like my own father, who directed me as a child and would have done so again, had he not…"

All the words get sucked from my throat. He *once* was kind. He *once* was a father. After my mother died, he rarely viewed me again as his child. Although he continued my training as an actress, he was drifting afar.

"It must have been so trying for you to go on in your life without anyone guiding you. How you have managed on your own, what strength you have had, I cannot imagine."

I catch my breath. Miss Coutts does not see me as a prostitute. Nor does Miss Jane. Perhaps that is why it is easy to speak to them. They view me as a girl, first and foremost. Mr. Dickens and the men see me as fallen, I am sure.

Miss Coutts studies my face, then examines my hair, now long enough to be pinned back without sticking up at odd angles. It's been flattened in place with cocoa-nut oil and emits a whiff of chocolate.

Her face brightens. "I believe you are a girl we can count on to succeed, Orpha. Mr. Dickens *will* lead you to the best possible solution, I am certain of it. Meanwhile, you and I will have our little secret."

As I rise to leave, she adds, "Your talents and training must not go to waste."

·· ● ··

At bedtime much later, I head to our room. My roommates are awake.

"Reading Miss Coutts a bedtime story?" Sesina teases, propped in bed. "You and her seemed thick as thieves today. She don't coop us up that long. What's she see in you, anyway?"

You can't trust Sesina. She says one thing but means another. Beauty and barbs, side by side.

I shove the argument back at her. "Miss Coutts enjoys literature. Is there another girl here who can read aloud to her?"

Let them do it then, I wish to add but don't.

Sesina's glance cuts up and down my dress. "Of all the girls, it's you she wants to talk to most. You're her pet. Soon as you're gone, she'll find another."

"You're someone's pet too!" Leah suddenly blurts out. "And *he* will dump *you* as soon as he's done with you."

Never have I heard Leah speak like this. She's always so reserved. We have been taught that educated ladies, the kind we are pretending to be, always think before speaking. But the look on Sesina's face is worth it. Her face aflame, she whirls away from us both.

•• ● ••

Leah finds me dusting the parlor the next morning. She tugs my arm, pulling me into an alcove behind the bookcases. Her eyes are bloodshot. She's been crying.

"Sesina knows my secrets inside out just as she knows yours. She's stolen them from us like a common sneak. I've tried to forget. But that girl picks at scabs."

"Won't you tell me what happened to you as a child?"

"The worst!"

My eyes fix on hers. "I know the worst."

She puts her fingers to her lips. "You keep your own stories to yourself. Promise you won't tell mine."

"I promise."

Her eyes suddenly harden into two pinpricks. "It was my father's thieving partner. Brought Pa home dead drunk late every Saturday. Ma was already asleep and Pa passed out. I did not scream. Petrified my father would beat me. It was something forbidden, what no one speaks of, so I never told anyone except Sesina and Mr. Dickens."

She pauses to take a deep breath. "It took me years to stop thinking of it every day. I've never felt clean enough, not even after a bath. His stealing fingers. His pushy body. The marks are on me yet."

I cry out, then squeeze her hand in mine.

"How brave you are, Leah, to tell me your story."

Afterward, I lead her outside so we can sit in the spring sun together, letting it warm us through and through to our bones. Her head leans against my shoulder and she shuts her eyes against the light.

Haven't I always sensed something about her? The way she tiptoes into a room as if fearful of entering. How she disappears in plain sight. How she cannot say no to Sesina. Leah lives more in the edges of the rooms than here with us. Just as I do.

·· ● ··

Every day, the garden gives delights. Today, the black hollyhock opens the petals of its face. For supper, we eat "earlies." Mrs. Marchmont insists that new potatoes are so edible, we need only serve them plain boiled with a pat of butter alongside a spring onion. In my mouth, the earlies squish softly, creaming my throat. Tomorrow we will harvest peas and radishes and bake rhubarb pie. I've wiggled my way to sit at dinner beside Alice, who leaves her shawl over the seat next to her, waiting for me.

·· ● ··

On Saturday night, the checks for good behavior are tallied up. "Name your reward, Orpha." The matron smiles. "Twenty marks total! You've saved all your earnings so far. Now, why don't you buy something special for yourself?"

"Ink."

"Ink?" Her eyebrows rise.

"I've been writing with dirt paste on old newspapers. You must have seen my muddy apron many a time."

The next afternoon, a bottle of ink sits on the kitchen table with a ream of old papers, used on one side, blank on the other. The ink is dark blue. It's the exact brand ordered for Mr. Dickens.

·· ● ··

At the very end of June, we awake early to a fuss in the dining room. The matron pounds down the stairs carrying a silver candlestick. We slide to the banister. Below, in the hallway, the matron dashes off a letter while Miss Jane stands shaking by her side.

"Hand this note to Dickens. None other than him," the matron orders the assistant. "If I could trust leaving that girl alone, I'd go myself. Awaken Zachariah and go!"

Miss Jane gasps. "Oh! What has happened?"

"Fanny found this in Jemima's bed this morning!" The matron points to the candlestick. "The nerve of that girl to steal!"

"Dickens!" Sesina hisses in my ear. "We're all in trouble now!"

She tiptoes back into our room, slips a hand beneath her mattress, and pulls out the bottle of gin, now half full. She wedges it behind the dresser where she keeps other things hidden.

"He'll be so batty when he comes, he'll search *all* our rooms!" Then she pleads. "Don't tell him! I could be kicked out."

From downstairs, Mrs. Marchmont shouts orders. "Shake the rugs out, Fanny! Orpha, there's dust on the tables! Alice, polish the furniture! Everything must be neat when he comes."

All that morning, Dickens's name hisses around the house. Hours pass. The matron removes a wardrobe of tattered clothing from a chest and hangs it up to air.

·· • ··

He flies into Urania like March wind, coattails lifting behind him. All girls except Jemima are ordered to line up in the parlor. His glance slides across the room and examines every piece of furniture. How odd his way of expecting each room to be shining as if set for a play.

Eyes bulging, spit flying, he now faces us. "Did any of you know of Jemima's plans to steal the candlestick?"

One by one, we all shake our heads. He squints, studying each of us head to shoe, lingering on our eyes. Glad I am to have polished my boots and turned my apron to the clean side.

"Was she planning to sneak away with it?" he now demands.

Something passes over Sesina's face, just a flicker. Mr. Dickens catches it too. He slides right in front of her.

"You knew what she was up to?"

"Oh, no, sir." Sesina curtsies at once. "It's just that she's always complaining there's too many rules here."

"Hmm!" Mr. Dickens fumes.

Up the stairs he thumps, opens the bedroom door and slams it.

"Please give me another chance, sir! I didn't mean to take it."

Then Mr. Dickens's voice: low, measured, and muffled.

Suddenly the door swings open. "Bring the dress!" he shouts.

The matron carries a raggedy gray dress, torn at the sleeve, and a threadbare shawl, upstairs to Mr. Dickens.

Now we hear him say, "Stealing is against the law. It's what sent you to prison in the first place. The committee has voted! Out you go!"

Screeching, very high-pitched. "Give me another chance!"

Mr. Dickens marches across the upper hallway, disappearing into our rooms. While Sesina taps her fingers on her thighs, the rest of us scurry like mice in all directions, pretending to be busy with tasks.

"Fanny!" he calls down. "Straighten up here at once!"

All eyes shift upward. None of us dare look at one another. The matron studies us closely, as does Miss Jane. More than ten minutes later, Fanny shakes her head at us from the landing, signaling that nothing was discovered. Sesina's shoulders drop.

Mr. Dickens stomps downstairs into the parlor. Back and forth he paces, hands behind him.

Jemima drags herself downstairs in her old bonnet and dress, following the matron. Miss Jane hands her some coins. One last time, Jemima swivels around to Dickens. He does not turn. She slams the front door behind her.

We rush to the front windows to watch Jemima go, wiping her face, her bonnet half sliding off. We girls clutch one another.

"Where will she go with only a few coins and dressed like that?" Alice sobs.

"I had to tell!" Fanny blurts out between tears. "That candlestick stuck right out of her mattress this morning."

"She got what was coming to her, didn't she?" Sesina shrieks.

"Poor thing!" The matron sighs, wiping her eyes. "If only she'd resisted temptation!"

In the parlor, Mr. Dickens slips behind the curtains and peeks outside. Jemima stumbles on the pathway, searching through her pockets. She shrugs her shoulders and walks off.

There's a sigh from behind the curtain. Mr. Dickens emerges, wiping his face with a handkerchief. He plops down in a chair, looking exhausted. The man is pure theater. He has just performed a matinee for all the girls to see. Shivering and tearful, they are, as an audience always is, watching high drama. He created a scene just for us. There isn't a girl among us who would dare think of stealing from now on. Isn't he the cleverest actor?

Dear Miss Wood,
July 10, 1857

I'd like to invite you to meet my family in London.

My driver, John Thompson, will fetch you in his carriage and drive you safely to Tavistock House, my London home. Miss Macartney can be your chaperone for the trip.

Shall we say the first Monday of August for tea? Most of my family will be in from the Country that day. We will be away from London most of this month.

Yours truly,
Boz

Hannah's voice hammers away. "Use your whole body to flatten that dough. Give it air … Orpha? You're not paying attention!"

"It's Mr. Dickens...he's asked—"

"He's got his ways. All men do. Don't pay attention to Sesina's complaints. Or call him names behind his back as Polly did. *His lordship*, she mocked him."

I stop kneading. "Does he invite *all* Urania girls to his home?"

Hannah nods. "He likes to ready us to go out on our own. Some bolt. Like that flighty Isabella last year. First chance she got. Never came back."

"Did you ever go to Tavistock, Hannah?"

Hannah throws back her wide shoulders. "Certainly I went. Even baked custard for his children. They devoured it as if nobody ever fed them. Made me proud!"

"But weren't you...afraid of being...on your own?"

"I was bent on seeing Dickens's home. Full of oak furniture, velvet drapery, too many rooms to count, and all those children! Why, the little ones even gave me a tour!"

Hannah covers the dough for rising.

"That man has a heart," she sighs. "When he found me, at sixteen, scrubbing Clerkenwell's stone floors, he cried to find out how I lost my mother. No one ever cried for me before."

Mr. Dickens does not expect custard from me. It's my story he's after. Last time we spoke, I gave him tidbits:

fish bait. He didn't press. Of that time past the cemetery, and well before, I cannot, will not, tell.

·· ● ··

In our darkened bedroom, hissing with candle smoke, Sesina is whispering. We crouch on either side of her.

"What would you two say if I told you I was leaving here?"

"You will! But I'm going first," Leah protests. "The matron says you'll sail after me in late spring."

"Well, I'm not waiting for that."

Sesina lifts her head to look out the window at the road in the distance, the one leading to London. Shivers run down my back.

"I'm running off. Soon as I can. You and I have been best friends for a year, Leah. Won't you come with me? I could teach you lots."

Leah tightens her lips. "I've got prospects in Australia. A real position! And maybe a chance to marry. All I want is to leave this country behind. And everything else too—"

Sesina studies Leah closely. Perhaps she has heard the venom snaking through Leah's voice, how she spits out her answer.

"All right." She sighs. "But I don't want to leave on my own. What about you?" Sesina turns to me, smoothing my hair in her fingers. "You don't want to be a nanny or a governess either. You're much too clever to be a maid."

Her hands clutch mine. "If you come with me, you'll be your own girl, Orpha. Do what you want. We know you've been writing. London's the best place for that. Theater. Books. Everything you want is there. Besides, Reuben's got plenty of boyfriends lined up for you."

Leah and I exchange a look. *How does she know my secret desires? Not like hers. Except for one thing: freedom to be myself.*

·· ● ··

For weeks after Jemima leaves, it is impossible to pass by Fanny's room without a peek inside at the empty bed, its soft pillow waiting. *If only Ivy would come! Haven't I asked and been given no answer, not even a single word in a letter?*

Downstairs, the trustees call July's committee meeting early. Fanny and Hannah plaster their ears flat to the door.

Inside, a voice rises: "Polly ran off once ashore in Australia! So says the very chaperone we hired to keep a close eye!"

Mrs. Marchmont clears her throat. "What shall we tell the girls?"

"Tell them nothing!" booms Dr. Brown.

"We can't do that," Reverend Illingworth says so softly that Fanny must mouth his words. "They hang on what the others do. We must cover it up—"

Mr. Dickens interrupts. "Tell them the letter was

sent to me. Say both arrived healthy. If anyone wishes more, let them come to me."

"They won't dare!" Chesterson shouts in a thunderous tone.

"Precisely!" Mr. Dickens agrees.

"Can you assure us that the next ones emigrating won't bolt, my dear Dickens?" Dr. Brown now inquires.

"The Hedgehog is a rather sturdy one. She will follow a straight path, as will the Little Mouse. As for Leah, she's a Lamb who follows."

Hannah grins proudly at that speech.

"Now, on to Urania's next recruit. Who's on the list?"

The voices blur. Name after name is said. I can't hear them all.

"Sarah?"

"In the darks for biting a matron. Not very promising news."

"Ivy?" My back straightens.

"Not to be released until August. Awaiting a behavior report."

"Martha?"

"She's the one at St. Pancras workhouse. Very young. I'll stop by there soon to see what she's like."

"We'll wait for the right girl," Chesterson announces. "A girl we can mold. Write to me by month's end what news you find."

So many names said. Did they linger more on one girl's name?

The matron's protesting voice next. "...you invited Orpha to your home, sir? She might be overwhelmed to be out in the world just yet. It's much too soon."

Mr. Dickens's loud voice heads straight my way as if he knows I am listening. "I beg to differ with you. The girl's been locked away in prison and now here. If we overshelter her, she'll never be ready for the real world once she leaves Urania."

"But, sir, how can you take the chance after Australia?"

"I insist on it. Let's see what Ophelia's made of!"

I bolt from the door, tumbling with a bang to the floor, forcing all the other girls to rush off. My whole body flushed when he said that name: *Ophelia!* A troubled girl who lost all her innocence. I knew whose nickname it was at once: it was mine!

·· ● ··

I run straight to the garden afterward, my throat pumping her name: *Ivy! If you don't come, I am lost. I'll have no true friend. What am I doing here without you?*

From across the miles, words ache to be said between us.

"Ivy! I can't wait for you any longer! Come!"

I must have been hollering, for Miss Jane raises the hall window and looks out. She sees a girl crying, her arms raised to the sky. She can't know that the girl is heaving her voice across the expanse that is England, all the way to a small cell on the north side of Tothill. Miss Jane gestures for me to come in for my interview at once.

·· ● ··

As I stand in front of him, her name still heats my lips. But I can't say it aloud. If I push too hard, he might never let Ivy come. So I let her name sit.

Besides, he is already lifting his white quill and dipping it.

"Do you feel ready to go on with your story? You were telling me last time how you ran from your aunt's house. Where to? How you ended up at Tothill, I would like to know."

I sit bolt upright and push the words out.

"I hid in a church cemetery near the west end of the rookery, sir. A forgotten place. Untended. Where dead flesh rots and molds in open graves and corpses are piled on top of one another with a shovelful of dirt. When it pours for days on end, the dead are uncovered. The stench is awful."

"Why did you pick such a forsaken place?" He busily jots it down in his book.

"I had nowhere else to go, sir. Come dark, I was hidden."

"How long did you stay?" he asks.

"Until winter's cold forced me out."

A reeking odor now fills the room: flesh rotting on decaying bones. Mr. Dickens raises his head at once. He jumps to his feet to pry open a window. As he sits back at his desk, his eyes widen.

"Your words give me great grief, Orpha. London teems with girls like you with no safe place to live. And still no one sees."

Not a word does he say about the stink that seeped into the room. It has vanished as if it never were here.

"Your story needs to be told." He glances up from the Case Book. "It can help heal you to share it with another soul."

Mr. Dickens swiftly writes as if his fingers are greedy to take my story down. He leans so far over the Case Book, he could almost fall into it. Urania's girls live in our confessions hidden in that book, kept under lock and key. No one has the power to open us but him.

I have closed my eyes to think about this.

"Ophel...?" Mr. Dickens's eyes light on me. "Ah... Miss Wood, will you join us soon at Tavistock? You never wrote back."

I find myself nodding. August is a long time to wait to see him again. Waiting is all I do. It has not brought

Ivy any closer. Sesina says she can't stay on longer. Why should I?

It is dusk now. The matron enters with a knock and lights the lamp, leaving Mr. Dickens in lamplight and me in the dark. I jam my lips together and lower my eyes so he cannot read me. Reverend Illingworth comes in to say he will lead our evening prayers now. I jump up at once to follow him out.

DICKENS'S CASE BOOK: NUMBER 98

How many Homeless girls creep into cemeteries and alleyways to hide from harm? Or worse, are found there, alone, with no one to shield them? Of the few we Rescued, even those we cannot always count a success. Nothing could be done to save Jemima. Likely we will hear of her at Coldbath soon.

It wasn't just her Wildness, as Chesterson insists, that spirited Polly away. What part was our own failure? The times she was difficult and foulmouthed—was I too hard on her? Did we judge wrong when we Pigeonholed her as a domestic? Perhaps her wildness needed a more Creative outlet. Now we will never know.

And then there's Ophelia. A great shame clouds her as it does me.

Do we ever heal our wounds? They dive so deep, away from the light.

I return from Shepherd's Bush this night, like Lot's wife, after she became a pillar of salt.

CD

One afternoon, all my chores done, I settle down on an old blanket in the coop. Nearby, Freckles clucks, pleased with her carrot peelings. A little window above my head gives a view to skywatch. Way up high, clouds form shapes that break apart just as I name what they look like: a bearded, scaled dragon with a high back and a goat stretching its legs to jump.

Images of Tothill pass through my mind just like those clouds: the young howling girl, A11, whose real name I will never know; a redheaded crown debtor last seen in the darks; and the suicide banished to Bedlam.

Leaning against the wall, breathing in and out, I listen to voices call from a far-off place. One must be very still to hear it. Suddenly, there's a tug, something shifting inside, ready to float to the surface. Tothill's girls speaking to me, Ivy among them. Fingers leap to write it down at once.

Dear Charles,

Your proposal for the next Urania recruit coincides with Miss Coutts's suggestion. It will be considered along with the rest of the proposals. This time, we must be sure of our girl and take no chances. God knows what we have to work with.

It is becoming disheartening, I must say. We never know for sure when these homeless girls might turn away from what we offer or which ones will do so. Even after a year's education, there is still no certainty. There is a wildness in many a street girl that propels her body before she uses her mind.

What is our success rate in rehabilitating them over all these years? I daresay not more than half the girls have success. Surely Miss Coutts could make a better investment in any other charity than Urania if she so chooses.

Your partner,
George Chesterson

TWELVE

Twirling in front of the hallway mirror, a young woman in a blue dress and bonnet, hair tucked neatly into a bun at the nape of her neck, looks back. She seems a lady on her way to afternoon tea in London.

At last, Thompson knocks at the door. "Afternoon, miss. I've come to drive Miss Wood and her chaperone to Tavistock."

In the next moment, Miss Jane and I are off. Lulled by the trotting of horse's hooves, my body rocks back and forth. Miss Jane's accustomed to carriage rides; she takes out a magazine to read. But the whole world suddenly appears in front of me and I have to stop myself from hanging my head out the window. Farms. A forever road. Cornfields.

Wide-open spaces are then swallowed by houses crammed together like crooked teeth in a mouth. Thompson swerves to avoid puddles and racing boys. Shouts and grinding wagon wheels fill the air along with whiffs of dung and piss, as we pass through London's narrow lanes thronging with crowds. Behind us, to the south, Tothill looms.

Men with broad backs pass by. The glance of a

stranger leaning in a doorway slices through me. I sink into a corner of the carriage. Someone from the rookery might recognize me. Some think me still in prison.

Luther may.

He doesn't give up easily. He had me trained. With just a nod, I slunk down before him like a beaten alley dog. The back of my bodice soaks with sweat.

"We're here, Orpha!" Miss Jane tugs my sleeve.

A uniformed maid, introducing herself as Anne, opens the door.

Above me, five curly heads peek between the banisters upstairs.

"She's here!" one boy shouts while the rest cheer.

Sweeping past them on the stairs must be Mrs. Catherine Dickens. She descends, hand on the oak banister, as if it took great deliberation. All lace, ruffles, and wide skirts, everything jiggles: her dark ringlets; full bosom; and her enormous waist.

"Come down, everyone. Miss Jane returns for a visit. Give her a nice bow. And meet my new charge: Miss Wood." Mr. Dickens stands beside me. "The one I told you about—the actress!"

As the boys barrel past her, his wife pauses, frozen as a butterfly pinned between two panes of glass. After introductions, she wanders away, leaving behind a strong odor of spices.

Alfred begs me, "Play with us! Our sisters are away in the country. Without them, we're always getting into trouble."

The tribe of boys drags me upstairs on a tour, just as Hannah said. I get a glimpse of their father's study, quiet and dim, and their own rooms with shelves and shelves of books.

"We make up our own beds ourselves." Alfred points. "Papa inspects them each morning. If we want playtime, we must be neat."

Their parents' bedroom is dark, with a dressing room at either end and an empty fireplace. A mirrored lowboy with a lady's chair. Hairbrush and pins lie upon it. The stopper of a bottle is flung there, fresh black drops on the doily as if someone had scurried away suddenly. An odor of nutmeg lingers in the air.

Downstairs, at the table, Mrs. Dickens is already pouring tea.

"So exciting for our boys to meet an actress. We often perform plays at Tavistock. Our children love to watch and memorize parts."

As if on cue, Plorn, the youngest, asks, "Are you a *real* actress?"

"It didn't take them long." Mrs. Dickens smiles between bites of fruitcake. "Our boys are not at all shy with strangers."

"Well, Miss Jane isn't a stranger!" Walter exclaims. "She always pays attention to our questions."

Miss Jane smiles at him. "Indeed I do. You boys have such inquisitive minds, I enjoy hearing what you have to say. Last time, we spent hours discussing your favorite books."

I turn to the youngest. "I was an actress in training once, yes, when I was very young like you. Both my parents acted."

"Our father acts." Plorn grins. "But not Mother."

"Indeed he does." His father laughs. "Most of the time, in fact!"

The parlor warms with laughter.

"Do you act in plays now?" Walter wonders.

"Well, I . . . do remember some speeches."

"Please! Give us one now!" begs Plorn, popping up in his chair.

"Let her enjoy her tea—" admonishes their mother.

Her husband cuts in. "How do we treat our guests, boys?"

"Politely, Father," Sydney, the quietest, answers. "We inquire of their health and their journey here. And don't bother them."

Mr. Dickens tilts his head back and roars. "Perhaps if you finish your tea, Miss Wood might treat you to a speech during playtime."

Silence spreads around the table. Plorn, yawning, soon gets up and cuddles in his mother's lap.

"Sweet boy!" She pets his head. In an instant, he falls asleep.

After our meal, Harry guides me out open glass doors to a balcony that feels like a stage. Walter hands me what he calls a disguise: a long white nightshirt. As it drapes over me, billowing in the breeze and lifting like wings, it is clear what speech I must perform. If I dare.

Perhaps I've buried my voice so deep, it might never speak again. But if I could practice here, safely among these children, it might be coaxed out of hiding. In the parlor, they won't even notice. Their father, head bowed, silently scribbles notes while Miss Jane embroiders in a world of her own, eyes downcast. Catherine slumps, chin to chest, as if she lived elsewhere.

Releasing my bun from its clip and mussing it with my fingers, I lean on the balcony and lift my voice.

And I, of ladies most deject and wretched,
That sucked the honey of his music vows,
Now see that noble and most sovereign reason
Like sweet bells jangled, out of tune and harsh;
That unmatched form and feature of blown youth
Blasted with ecstasy. Oh, woe is me,
To have seen what I have seen, see what I see!

"O-phel-i-a!" Walter shouts.

That name echoes from each boy's lips.

"*Ophelia!* I knew it. She's playing Hamlet's betrothed." Plorn awakens with a shout, running out to the balcony. "Do it again!"

I repeat Ophelia's speech and follow it with another. That speech is like a door creaking wide open. Beyond it, hundreds of speeches line up, all shouting to be heard. I recite Hamlet's soliloquies next, known by heart, listened to over and over, as a child hidden in the wings: parts I never knew I had memorized; speeches that never passed my lips before. Words fill me to the brim and illuminate the balcony. They even still the wild boys, who sit rapt and quiet before loudly applauding when I finish.

Across the room, Mr. Dickens's head shoots up and our eyes meet in a kind of conspiracy. *Ophelia!* He's heard me recite before, but never has he watched a character live and breathe through me. My whole body flushes. *What I am, I always was. It never left me! He sees it too!*

We stay until evening while the light still lingers soft and yellow, brightening the streets leading back to Urania. Miss Jane talks on and on, telling stories of the boys, but I am wrapped in my own thoughts. Of Tavistock, I wonder how Mr. Dickens gets any writing done amid his lively boys. Of his marriage, I sense great distance. It is as if Mr. Dickens sits in his own cell at Tothill and his wife in hers.

And of myself, I know at last that my voice has no boundaries. It can fly equally across a theater or a room, awakening the hearts of the young and old. It's the truest part of me. Didn't my pa always say so?

Dear George,

Much can be known about a person from just listening to their voice. Today, from where I write to you at Tavistock, I hear Miss Wood playacting for the amusement of our children. Her sure voice shoots across the summer breeze, each word delivered like a punch. I hear such Grieving in it.

Ophelia is aptly named.

My hope is that she will Endure even in this Heartless city where, every day, at every hour, girls are thrown away.

For you see, it is not statistics we should worry about, but the possibility of the Transformation of even one lost soul.

Sincerely,
Charles Dickens

"What a fine speech you made of Ophelia!" Mr. Dickens compliments me in Urania's parlor the following week. "Perhaps now we should discuss if you've given thought to other work Dr. Brown suggests you are best suited for?"

"A governess, sir? I've never been around children."

"Any child would listen to you, easily. Indeed, my own children were completely captivated. They keep begging me to invite you back."

My sigh fills the space between us.

"If you could be anything"—he tilts his head—"what would it be?"

"I once hoped to be an actress, sir."

Now Mr. Dickens's sigh is heard. "It's not easy to be one in London. I know of an acting family here, the Ternans, a widowed mother with three girls, careful of their reputation, always traveling together, taking only conservative roles in plays."

"Why should that be, sir?"

"A woman must be sheltered by a man's name or else her standing could be ruined by one misstep. *Especially* if she is an actress. In England, an actress is viewed suspiciously—just as if she were a fallen woman!"

"Does the whole world think like London?"

"Paris admires its artists and survivors. That city forgives women who drift into prostitution. When destitute, women have few choices to support themselves.

Yet many are capable of improving their lives if given another chance."

"Surely Mrs. Dickens has freedom? She is married!"

He laughs. "Heaven forbid! There must be a chaperone or footman and carriage with her at all times. And her dress plain, not attracting attention."

Marriage alone offers shelter for women; it turns us into statues upon a shelf, like Mrs. Dickens. Yet Mr. Dickens goes where he pleases and does what he wishes.

"What if I...if I could possibly become a writer like you, sir?"

He shakes his head at once. "Society will never accept writing from a fallen girl. If you used your real name, you'd be traced to Tothill. That would be scandalous."

"But, sir, women novelists sell their work in London!" I protest. "Elizabeth Gaskell, the novelist, wrote a story of prostitution in your own magazine, *Household Words*. I've read it in Urania's library."

"Such a woman is deemed respectable—meaning she has a name, family, and money. And a husband too!"

I meet his answer with a scowl. I will never have those things.

Instead, my destiny is to be a governess, a kind of servant. Mistress of nothing. Unless I marry and lose myself altogether. Perhaps that's why Sesina longs for a fancy dress, one of taffeta and ruffles—the first thing she'll get once she leaves here, she tells us, "to make my mark."

At the end of our interview, Mr. Dickens and I stand shoulder to shoulder at the open window admiring the summer roses, whose myrrh perfume wafts into the room. Side by side, we are of equal height. Yet we are not equal, nor could we ever be.

I think of the young girls he might pass tonight, walking the midnight streets with bold legs and bare heads, the sort that end up at Tothill. Yet for Mr. Dickens, the night is an adventure, his "magic lantern," as he calls it, to roam freely and alone. How I wish I could be him!

·· ● ··

Miss Coutts appears in crisp pale linens, wide-brimmed bonnet, and thin white boots, an outfit that looks as though it could outsmart this day, the hottest day of the summer. She waves a letter like a fan in the air.

"We are applying overseas for positions for you and Ivy," she says.

"Ivy! Did you hear from her?"

"Not only have I heard from her, but she has heard from us. It's all been arranged. Your friend arrives at Urania tomorrow."

It is impossible to stay in my seat after that. As Miss

Coutts tells me the details—the letters back and forth, the interview, the approval of the committee, and the final say both she and Mr. Dickens had—my feet dance around her just as Fanny might, not ladylike at all.

"You did this because I asked after Ivy?"

"Ivy is a good candidate. Mr. Dickens believes she is very forthright and will make her way anywhere if given a chance. And, besides that, we both feel strongly that friendship will help you develop trust and feel safer when you emigrate together. Your concern for Ivy's future impressed us both."

The urge is to hug her. Instead, I curtsy low as I would at the theater.

"I am delighted that you are so pleased, Orpha!" Her usually serious face lights up. "Ivy has delayed writing you about this, she told me. She was fearful we'd reject her. But, I assure you, she *is* coming!"

I run outside to my chores. All the way out to the garden, the hot oven exhales the scent of baking bread. How sweet it is then to pluck red globes of beets, and carrots like plump orange fingers out of the earth. Tomorrow, Ivy will sit beside me at the table—beets, carrots, and bread delighting her mouth.

·· ● ··

The next day is heavy with heat, sun blaring, when Ivy steps into the parlor. She stumbles on a rug, so busy she is, scanning the polished room. She's smaller and paler than I remember. A halo of black curls frames her tiny face.

"They told me Orpha would be here," Ivy says. "Where is she?"

"She's right here," I say quietly.

Ivy immediately turns, her eyes lingering on my hair.

"It's you!" she gasps. "I never imagined your hair so thick and brown. You look healthy and happy. Not like at Tothill."

Hannah roars. "Most of us looked like we cracked straight out of an egg when we first came here from prison!"

The girls giggle and point at one another. Beside me, Sesina mutters, "Thought we were your best friends, but now there's another."

"You're here." I reach out my hands, stepping toward Ivy.

We entwine our fingers and swing our arms back and forth like children, teasing a shy smile from Ivy. Her eyes are so wide, they light up her whole face.

·· ● ··

At bedtime, in Fanny's hushed room, the windows are still closed against the heat of the day. Fanny opens the windows wide, letting in the evening breeze. The curtains lift and twirl and dance.

Ivy turns her head to watch, taking a deep breath. "Oh!"

I point out her side of the room, where a white

nightgown is laid on the newly crocheted bedspread. Tears slide down Ivy's face.

"Why, it's all made up, just for me," she cries. "A real bed!"

"I'll help you get ready for sleep. Lights out soon."

Ivy grabs my hand. "Don't leave me, Orpha. Stay!"

Fanny shrugs. "Fine with me. Been awfully quiet since my last roommate got booted out."

Ivy changes into the nightgown, her back turned. Suddenly I am not at Urania anymore. Tothill's stone walls slam between us with a chill, all that silence and separation. There were only her eyes to tell me, like a flame, that I was still alive.

She turns around then, reaching out, pulling me close, without a word. Together, we lie on the narrow bed, my arm encircling her thin waist, my stomach flat to her back, as if we had both just hatched.

"I'll stay, Ivy. Soon, we'll talk about everything."

Ivy closes her eyes. My breath falls in time with hers. I don't feel my body anymore, only hers. *She's here. She's safe.* The chant sighs back and forth between us like a sleeping potion.

·· • ·

In the middle of our arithmetic lesson the next day, all heads turn toward Ivy. Everyone's mouths drop open. All except Sesina's. Her eyes glitter hard as flint.

Fanny gasps. "Ain't she something? She can add piles of sixpence and shillings in her head without using her fingers!"

"She could be a banker, that one!" Hannah says.

"Or a coiner." Sesina smiles slyly.

Hannah blurts out, "She's a counterfeiter?"

Ivy reddens from all the attention.

Mr. Dickens arrives late in the afternoon, wiping his neck with a handkerchief. His shirt billows at his waist and he's forgotten to comb his hair. He carries an odor of violets into the house, sweet and somehow sickly.

"Why, Mr. Dickens, don't tell me you walked *all* the way here!" Miss Jane exclaims. "On such a hot day too!"

He brushes past her. "If I couldn't walk this far, I should just explode!"

In the parlor, I notice it immediately: fingers tapping on the desk; eyes staring blankly at the floor; and his breathlessness. *He's elsewhere!*

"Where were we?" He clears his throat at the start of our interview.

"You were about to…tell me…how…to write, sir? You said I should take notes. I am doing so."

He turns to me then as if awakened from a dream.

"Not many yearn to know how it's done. Or are as curious as you, Ophelia."

He does not hear my nickname drop from his lips.

"An educated girl should also keep a journal. Remind

me next time to speak of that. Tell me what else you have been doing."

"The readings are going well, sir," I tell him. "The girls hang on every word you wrote. You capture people and make them real."

His head lowered, his quill circling the Case Book without landing. "Perhaps it is your speaking voice that charms them most!"

"Who could not love Oliver and hate the Artful Dodger, even as we admire his tricks? How do you make them come alive on the page?"

"Hmm... they have to set foot in your own mind first and dwell there. Do you know someone who does that for you?"

Many, I want to answer him.

He lifts his head. "Can you hear their voice *inside* you? Hearing someone speak gives clues to their character."

Mr. Dickens's voice is as crisp as his fine suits. But Rose's voice shrank as she sickened; she stopped singing.

He narrows his eyes. "Whom did you think of just now?"

"Rose... I can't get her out of my thoughts."

Mr. Dickens shuts his eyes. "Begin like a painter. Small brushstrokes. Then come in closer with telltale details that reveal a whole story. Broken nails. Collar askew. Stains on the bodice. Drips of pus and blood. Eyes wide and startled."

Between us, he is conjuring Rose.

"Do you mean I must *see* first before writing?"

"Exactly. Allow your character to come alive before you commit to one word."

I gasp. "If I could set Rose on a page, maybe she'd stop haunting me."

"Let me warn you." He sighs. "Writing is both cure and curse. It never lets you be. If you wish to become a writer, you must press yourself into it, body and soul."

"Body and soul, I already gave away, sir."

It happens quickly the moment those words are said—Luther's face forms. His broad nose flattened by tavern fights. The tiny black spokes of his pupils sharpening when I was cornered. The glittering blade squeezed tight in his fist. My hands fly to cover my face.

I never told anyone about the Valentin, with its sleek, double-edged blade. "Slices through a stomach and grinds it around," Luther boasted. "Yanks out your innards in a minute."

"You are a story within a story, Miss Wood." Mr. Dickens leans forward. "Someday soon, I hope, you will tell me all of it."

A whole hour passes and not one word of my story has he written down. Instead, his chin cupped in his hands, his gaze straight on me, we talk endlessly about how he writes his books. He does not guess I am memorizing his ways. Not clay to mold; but a sponge to absorb.

DICKENS'S CASE BOOK: NUMBER 98

Orpha is Ice and Fire. Somewhere between the two, she must land. So many girls let the fire consume them. We have had more than our share at Urania. Many were shown the door as Jemima was.

Sesina has such a fire that we must constantly keep her in check. But some never break through their frozenness either. Leah and Alice are such girls, in Constant need of Mrs. Marchmont to prop them up.

Orpha's fire is deep; her ice melting. She has only to use that spark and not let it consume her.

Give me a girl with anger rather than sadness. She has the Energy to change her entire life.

CD

Mornings, I rush straight to Ivy's room, lay out her outfit, and lead her down to breakfast as if she needed help.

During the day, when she passes by doing her chores, her hand reaches out to mine, giving it a soft squeeze.

We survived, her touch tells me. *We're together. At last!*

·· ● ··

One evening, after lingering late in Ivy's room, I step into our bedroom. Leah is already asleep but Sesina is sitting on my bed, filing her nails.

"I wouldn't bother with her, if I was you."

"Why not?"

"Ivy won't last at Urania. She's already stolen some lace from the supplies, did you notice? She's used to better, I can tell. And there's only one way for her to get that—thieving or lying on her back. Either way, she'll be back at Tothill."

I shoo her off my bed.

"You could have it all if you come to London with me," Sesina boasts. "If you stick with her, you'll just find trouble."

·· ● ··

Alice is absent from meals. Throughout the night, the whole house awakens to her constant coughing.

Leah prepares a dinner tray of soup and rolls and I carry it to Alice. In her bed, Alice seems to have shrunk down. Her chest barely lifts.

"I fear I will never leave England," she moans, "to feel that hot Australian sun they've promised me. Or ever forget losing my dignity."

"Don't upset yourself, Alice. Soon you will emigrate with Hannah. Try not to worry when you are so sick."

Alice stares out the window, as if seeing far away to London's past.

"What little I made from needlework did not take care of Ma and me. When we could no longer afford lodgings, Ma went to a refuge for the aged. I had nowhere to go. So I slept on stoops and in alleyways."

"Couldn't you get work? Your sewing is so fine."

"Without a bath or clean clothes, ladies shut their door when I came calling. Once, when I was waiting on a doorstep for work, the maid left the door ajar. I stole a book from the table and sold it for my supper."

"What happened?"

"They reported me! I was sentenced to three months at Coldbath. Dickens found me afterward in my parish.

"One thing he asked of me," Alice whispers between coughs, her handkerchief flecked with blood. "Has he asked it of you? If I ever lost my virginity."

"What did you answer?"

"I told the truth. Though I stole to eat, I was never corrupted by a man." She pauses to catch her breath before reaching out for my hand. "Tell him everything, Orpha...even if it hurts."

It's very dark when I awaken out of deep sleep to the sound of banging. Sesina stands at the open window, carpetbag in hand.

"Don't!" Leah yells, yanking her back.

"Shush! He's here, and I'm going."

Sesina lifts one foot out the window and then the other, her head disappearing. Below, Reuben is looking up as Sesina slowly descends the ladder he's steadying. She gasps and teeters as the ladder shifts, then falls into Reuben's arms.

"No time for that now. Let's go!"

Sesina smirks up at us and waves. Together, they sneak around the side of the house, dragging the ladder behind them.

"Shall we run downstairs and tell?" Leah whispers in a tiny voice. "They could bring her back."

I fold my arms across my chest. "She wanted to go. Besides, she's broken the rules. What would the committee say?"

Leah sighs. "They'd kick her out. At once! But if we don't tell now, what do we say in the morning?"

"We'll say we awoke and she was gone, the window wide open. We supposed her downstairs already. And when she's not—"

"You can lie like that?"

"Won't it be the truth?"

"You're clever, Orpha."

"I know how to keep secrets, that's all."

Leah grabs my hand. "Then swear you won't tell and we'll both stick to our story."

I swear it.

·· • ··

The next morning, Mrs. Marchmont rushes to the yard where Zachariah's ladder was dragged, leaving tracks in the dirt.

"A girl's gone! This has never happened on my watch before!" she exclaims, dashing off a letter. "If I call for the constable now, all of Shepherd's Bush will know what Urania really is. So I'll wait for Dickens to decide."

We pace on tiptoe all afternoon. Leah rehearses her lines over and over like an understudy in training. I tell her she must be firm, for Mr. Dickens can always pick out a liar. Mrs. Marchmont passes by, a handkerchief to her flushed face and neck, as she paces through the rooms.

This time, Mr. Dickens does not come running; he sends a letter instead. Miss Jane reads it aloud to the matron, her voice startled:

Don't bother the Constable. If the girl cannot resist temptation within the safe walls of Urania, then there is no hope for her. I don't want her back.

CD

·· ● ●··

We wait all day for the evening to come. Ivy's belongings are moved into Sesina's side of the room after Mrs. Marchmont agrees to our pleading to be together.

An impossible distance apart before, half an arm's length in line, yet untouchable, now we stretch our arms out to one another as we lie in our beds. Shoulders hanging off, we reach and reach until our fingers almost touch. Ivy topples to the floor, belly-laughing. I yank her back up to her bed.

Across the room, Leah yawns, extinguishing the candle. Ivy lifts her covers and beckons me over, finger on her lips. Slipping between the cool sheets, like a letter into its envelope, the two of us stay awake that whole night together, whispering in the dark until the sky brightens.

"Word spread in Tothill that a baby murderer was coming. That's the worst! When I looked at you, how haunted you seemed. Someone killed your spirit, is what I saw."

We lie face-to-face, stroking each other's hair.

"If only we could have spoken freely there." I sigh. "How much easier it would have been to do the sentence."

Ivy shakes her head. "Your face was all I had to read. You recognized my pain and showed me your own suffering too. For that, I loved you."

Her warm eyes look into me, to what I have been holding.

There are circles that bind you to people, linked like chains. Some are clamped upon you like Luther's iron grip on me. Ours, Ivy's and mine, entwine like vines, climbing higher together than they would have grown on their own.

The story falls out with words I believed would scorch my throat with fire and choke me like vomit. But when they pass out of me, it feels right and true, as if I'd saved them just for her.

Ivy's tears begin to fall well before I tell of Luther. By the time I'm done, she has drenched a week's worth of handkerchiefs. Afterward, she hugs me so close, her heart racing against mine, I cannot tell whose heart is whose, whose arms hold the other tighter, whose tears are falling, hers or mine.

"You weren't a criminal like me, Orpha. I broke the law again and again to get what I wanted. But terrible wrong was done to you and that led to other things." Ivy strokes my face. "I hope you told Dickens so. It's a relief to finally tell someone. Did you?"

"I told no one. Only you."

"You must tell it to *him*! So you can put Luther behind you. Why didn't you? Is it because you're ashamed?"

I nod.

"I told Dickens everything. Even plotted to do so, betting he'd help me find my boyfriend. He promises to send me to Tasmania because I am so sure of Jack. If he can find him. Dickens says people can change after such a shock—being arrested and transported like that. That's what I want for Jack."

"When did you tell Mr. Dickens your story?"

Ivy shrugs. "At Tothill. First thing he wanted was a confession. So I figured if I gave him what he asked right off, he'd do the same for me. I took a chance he'd bring me to Urania, and to you. And he has."

Never could I calculate like Ivy to get one small thing of my own.

Ivy grabs my hands. "Dickens promised we could become someone new and start all over again once we confess. Isn't that what you want too?"

·· • ··

The next day, Ivy and I gather herbs for fall harvest: spearmint in armfuls; bee balm for tea; and rosehips, round and rosy, laying them all out to dry on the back porch for winter's tea. My feet step as lightly as if they touched air, not ground. I follow Ivy as if we were still walking in line. Today, for the very first time, I actually see her smile. It softens her whole face. Girls like us can heal, Miss Jane believes. It's what Mr. Dickens says too.

I gave my secrets away. To her. In return, she's given her tears, falling on me like grace.

Next to Ivy, Urania's girls seem ordinary. Gossiping and fussing. Always abuzz. Hissing like snakes. Or clucking like hens. They can say the cruelest things. Even Sesina could be sweet before she suddenly turned on you, dropping your secrets like dirty laundry in front of everyone. Ivy will be true. We shared a foothold in Hell and held on tight together.

·· ● ··

All that week, Ivy and I take turns watching over Alice, who does not stay awake long. Sleep seems a potion she is drowning in, her chest lifting like a bird's breast.

When Alice finally awakens one afternoon, she pushes herself up in bed on thin arms. "Bring me my sewing bag. And your old dress, Orpha. I'll teach you both how to make a dress pattern on a new bolt of cloth."

We lay out my dress on her bed, pull the stitches apart, and lay each piece, the bodice, sleeves, and skirt, on a roll of plum bombazine, just as she instructed. When we turn around for our lesson, Alice is asleep, her mouth fallen open.

·· ● ··

Mr. Dickens arrives very late some days later, his eyes unfocused, collar askew and locks of hair sticking straight up as if he had rushed away suddenly. There's that scent again—stronger this time—of violets violently crushed and pressed against him.

I step back from him. The scent is cloying.

When the matron approaches with a list of Urania's bills, he plops down in the nearest chair.

"There, there, Mr. Dickens, you look as if you need a good rest!" She shoos us from the room.

"Dickens is like a housefly today," Fanny hisses, brushing past me. "Flitting from this to that. Not landing on a single thing."

Hannah corners me in the kitchen. "What's happened to Dickens? He's all flummoxed and comfoozled!"

An hour later, he grabs my elbow, leading me away. "No interviews tonight. *Please!*" he mutters. "I'm late with a novel installment and must pack for a three-week tour. And I cannot find my speech. Help me look."

In the back parlor, he rummages through the desk without finding it, then rushes out quickly at dusk to take the last evening train home, asking me to tidy up behind him.

Inside the glass case, the Case Book sits on a shelf, maroon leather beckoning. Mr. Dickens once called himself a "rag-and-bone man," a common street scavenger, plucking stories from everyone. Is he turning me into a character as he did with Alice? If I could peek inside the Case Book, I'd know. My life is set down in that book but it is not true. It is only the story of what he thinks my life was. I rattle the lock but it does not budge.

On the desk, his private journal lies open in plain view. He's never left it behind before. It's too late to call him back, for the train whistle has already screeched. My fingers touch the paper, still wet with blue ink. The page is crumpled in one corner as if his fist clutched it hard:

I am here, there, everywhere. There has not been a moment's peace since I met her in August. Nelly is the one spirit I thought I lost long ago.

Catherine and I are not meant for one another. Never were.

·· ● ··

Miss Coutts visits the next morning. The details of her dress escape me, as do her words. How I wish to tell her what I just learned of Mr. Dickens. She once said she hoped to be a friend, my confidante. How sweet to tell her of Ivy. But I can't tell her *this*. I was snooping.

If I don't think of it, it never happened.

·· ● ··

In the weeks that follow, Mr. Dickens disappears on tour in England, Scotland, Ireland, where he reads aloud to audiences. Thousands flock to him, I hear. He's even read to Queen Victoria. Always he carries fire into any room he enters.

I should know.

All those times, I sat down and warmed myself by him. But now he carries the spirit of another with him. One called Nelly. Not his wife, Catherine. My whole body is chilled.

DICKENS'S CASE BOOK: NUMBER 98

She may well have drifted into Thievery and Prostitution. Many a girl must do so in order to survive in this harsh city.

One thing I sigh in Relief of. I have finally located hospital records of Orpha's admission with a dead baby still attached to her. The Autopsy report, written months after the trial, termed the baby premature. A doctor I consulted said that most likely, the girl being so very young and malnourished, the baby was a Miscarriage, born dead, not the result of infanticide. No one thought to forward this report to Tothill, where it would have reduced her sentence.

No one spoke for her in Court either. While she may have wished herself and her baby dead, she did not take the path some do. We hear of their swollen bodies fished out of the Thames.

CD

For weeks, we've been indoors with driving rains. Mrs. Marchmont hands me a note from Mr. Dickens, the first communication from him all month.

"The play's the thing!" Mr. Dickens quotes Shakespeare, inviting me to a performance at Tavistock. "My friend Wilkie Collins is writing a new play, *The Woman in White*, and we are helping him stage a rehearsal in my home to see how it works. Come watch the acting with Miss Macartney, stay the weekend here with the actors. If you wish, join us for a scene. Miss Coutts will be here too."

"*Yes!*" I write back to him immediately.

Early next morning, Mr. Thompson arrives. "We must make a stop first—to deliver these letters of invitation to the new girls—at Tothill."

Tothill! The name stops my breath: the rookery, Devil's Acre on its rim, where Luther is still at large. My blue dress and bergamot-scented hair are not enough of a disguise. *I could be seen!*

The matron bustles over to me. "Orpha! Our Jane was called away quite suddenly by family matters. You can't travel alone in the carriage. It's hardly proper. By the time I write Mr. Dickens of it, it will be too late for you to go. Another time, perhaps—"

"I can't miss the play. It's my one chance to act again. Please let me go!" I rush away. "I'll be back in a minute."

In my ears, Jemima's words clang like Westminster bells: *Track him down! Chiv him good! Deep in the belly!*

I head straight to the kitchen to choose what I need— the long steak knife, freshly sharpened to slice through the flesh of lamb—and wedge it between ankle and boot. I bustle past the matron, who shakes her head but allows me to leave.

All through the journey, the air hangs damp and heavy. Coal smoke sneaks inside the carriage. Coughs gag my throat. The closer we get to Tothill, the more my mind scatters. It spreads all over the rookery in a million memory pieces, seeking safety, until it settles on one person: Emma. Perhaps I'll catch a glimpse of her. *Does she still think of me or is it too late?*

At last, Mr. Thompson halts the carriage. "Shan't be long, miss. Wait here."

Before me, Tothill looms like an ancient castle, facing north. Which room was mine up there and who lives in it now, I wonder. At this early hour, inmates will file down to the oakum room. Rose or Edwina may pass by in the hallway. Surely Hester still lingers.

My hand clutches the metal handle of the carriage door and my boot is about to slip out when the stink of sewer floats past. A man is slowly climbing Tothill's steps one at a time, almost toppling, then slowly steadying himself. He stops near the top, to watch and wait. It's a barrel-chested figure in dark and tattered clothes, hands sunk into pockets, legs planted wide apart like tree stumps. My breakfast rises to my throat.

He's come: *Luther!*

There could be only one reason he's standing there like that: he's looking for *me*. He must have seen girls released each morning and searched for my face among them, the Valentin in his pocket.

He's come for me!

I lift my voice to scream, then cover my mouth at once. My chest is heaving with screams and my heart pumps loud and hard like a fist.

If he turns around…if he walks down the steps…if he looks my way and sees me staring out the carriage window… My fingers fall to the cold blade of the steak knife. It seems too heavy to lift. I can barely breathe. Dropping to my knees, pressed to the floor, I curl into a ball, like Jonah in the belly of the whale.

Then, swiftly, the coal smoke shapeshifts into yellow fog smothering everything. The air thickens. Only the top of the building is still clear.

Tothill is swallowed by fog.

I can't see him anymore.

Suddenly, the carriage creaks sideways. Someone plops down heavily in the driver's seat and snaps a whip. The horses jolt and clomp away from Tothill. Back and forth I shift on the floor like a sack of flour, as the carriage turns left, then sharply right. I tell myself to grab the door handle to jump out, but my body won't budge.

I must get away!

"We're off!" It is only Mr. Thompson shouting to me.

My body never rises from the floor. Behind me, Luther still stands guard as he always did.

·· ● ··

I stand shivering in Tavistock's entrance. My cloak is damp and so is my bonnet. Specks of coal from the fog have settled onto my shoulders and gloves. Grease tracks mar my face. Anne lets me in with a gasp.

Inside, in an unlit corner of the hallway, a figure sits so still and motionless, it gives me a start. It seems a statue. Mrs. Dickens does not look up; she stares vacantly into space, her hands idle in her lap.

Anne puts her arm around me, turning me away from her mistress to lead me up the high staircase.

"Poor little miss, looks like you've had quite a shock! Whatever has happened? Come to my mistress's room for some dry clothing."

Their room is altogether different; it's been boarded off into two separate bedrooms: one for a man and one for a woman. The scent of nutmeg emanates everywhere in Catherine's side of the room. Now I can place it. That was the scent on the women's breath at the end of the night at Silver Feathers, their feet so unsteady they had to be guided up the brothel stairs, after swallowing their black drops. Afterward, they slept for long hours.

As I wish to do.

I rummage through the dresser drawers until I find the little blue bottle, wrapped tightly inside a shawl. The scent is pungent. Alcohol and spice. I can almost taste it without even opening the bottle.

My head spins. I see the two women clearly.

The madam leaning on me, mumbling to herself, out of her body, out of her mind; and Mrs. Dickens, sitting alone downstairs. That same faraway look. That same limp body.

Both betrayed by a man. One fallen. One discarded. Ruined.

My glance falls on the mirror above the dresser. Orpha stares back: her impeccable dress; her hair in disarray; her startled face.

She may be fallen.

She was betrayed, too.

She certainly was discarded.

But I am not ruined. Not like these two women.

I am not alone either. There are Urania and Ivy. And…there's Mr. Dickens right now, just outside the door, calling for me…

Quickly I slip the bottle back inside the drawer and change into a clean gown, shoving my knife into my carrying bag, then rush out the door.

Miss Wood arrives with a Haunted look.

"Poor child," Anne notified me at once. "She has visited her Ghosts this day."

Minutes later, Anne stops me on the threshold of his office.

"Nobody goes in there when he's like that. You must wait now, miss."

Inside, by the far window, Mr. Dickens sits at his desk in the last light of the day. His sleeves are rolled up and he is without a jacket. He leans forward, quill sailing across the page at gale speed, so still except for his one hand.

Contained, as if within a sheet of glass, he cannot see around him, only the world of his own imagination, while downstairs, in the hallway, Catherine slumps on a settee with unworked needlework upon her lap, in a spell of gloom.

For Dickens, solitude is like stepping into familiar clothes. No wonder his wife keeps black drops in her dresser. She has nowhere else to go.

But I do! I want to rattle the door, smash through the glass, open my mouth wide and scream.

Voices shout in my head. Some of them are mine.

Fool you were to think him gone! Luther did not have to knock on Urania's door. He does not come in ways you expect. Or open any door to enter a room. That room is inside you and therein he dwells. No matter where I am, I live there with him.

"Tell him everything, even if it hurts!" cries Alice's thin voice.

Even Ivy has a say. "Dickens promised we could become someone new and start all over again once we confess. Isn't that what you want too?"

·· ● ··

I have been watching him closely for an hour. He has finally paused for many minutes to stare out the window.

"Help me, sir!" I call to him. "Luther is looking for me!"

His head jolts up.

"Come in, dear girl. I've been waiting to speak with you. Whatever happened to you on your way here? Thomas could not explain it to us."

He does not let go of his quill.

"Sir! Today, I saw the man who binds me...on Tot-hill's steps...where he's waited for me all this time. He is my uncle...Luther!"

His groan fills the space between us. He motions me to sit.

If I'm to get the words out, the ones jamming my throat, I must not look at his face, only his hands. They are manicured and slender.

"I was not yet thirteen when put under his care. Too soon, at night...my aunt asleep...Luther's fingers roamed. Brushing the buds of my breasts no one ever touched before."

Mr. Dickens's free hand forms a fist as he writes with the other.

"Then I bled. That's when the worst began. In the middle of the night, I woke to him in my cot, his whis-kered face too near, his huge hand smothering my mouth and...his...bare body rubbing against mine."

My breath comes in jagged sips now. The quill squeaks without pause.

"It kept up. Sometimes for nights he did not come and then suddenly he did. His fingers roughly poking me between my legs 'to get you ready,' he said. And then one night, though I kicked and shoved...he pressed some-thing into me and there was such pain I thought I would die and be broken forever. But I did not die. Instead, I lived to see it happen again and again.

"Not one word did I tell. The knife was at my throat, sir! Then my monthly bleeding disappeared and I did not guess why. Perhaps he'd stopped it with the pain he gave me, I believed. Mornings, I bolted into the street to vomit.

"My aunt shouted, 'I might have guessed. Your secrecy. Your paleness. Sick every morning. You're with child, are you not?'

"I shook my head. Even then, I did not understand."

Mr. Dickens leans forward, mouth fallen open, and looks through me as if awakened from a nightmare. I turn away.

"She beat me and when done, she rolled my belongings into a ball and threw them into the alley. Straight to the cemetery I ran to hide. If it weren't for the prostitutes, I would have had nowhere to go that winter. I cooked and cleaned at Silver Feathers. Never did I step into the street, for fear of Luther. Until that man, their regular customer, cornered me.

"His fermented breath stank of gin. That man was always full corned, just like Luther, straight from the tavern. One day at the brothel, he wrapped his arms around my waist and pulled me to him—'Let me warm up with this young'un.' Behind his back, he never felt the madam's delicate fingers tooling his wallet. For that, he came after me. I had no choice but to bolt."

"He chased me through icy streets. I had a hard fall on wet cobblestones, a pumping in my belly pushing up to my throat. From between my legs, wetness gushed and I ran again until I dropped. When I awoke in a pool of blood, constables stood over me and that man was screaming about his wallet."

Mr. Dickens stops writing. Silence fills the room. His head drops upon the table and his hands thrash through his strewn hair.

Oh, what have I said, what sins and what horrors have I unleashed here in this fine house?

From between his clenched teeth comes a deep moan. And then, slowly, he lifts his head to look at me, his eyes very wide and dark. Suddenly, a tear drops down his face, big, and so bitter, I can almost taste it.

"Dear, dear girl!" he whispers. "You have been sorely used by those who should have cared for you. I should have known but dared not guess."

All the breath leaks out of me. "The baby, sir! In the hospital...they swore I did something terrible to it! But I can't remember."

"My child, I never had the chance to tell you what I learned just recently. The baby was not born alive. Indeed, it was not fully formed. The theft you have explained. So you are innocent of all charges. Dreadful I feel not to have had proof soon enough to free you from Tothill."

Shimmers ripple over my body. Heat waves in my belly.

Leave me! I told it over and over again. *I am not fit to mother you! Better you go!* It would have been impossible to hide with a baby or run fast enough. Sooner or later, he'd find us.

Suddenly I remember. When I awoke on the cobblestones, the baby was blue, its tiny fists clenched as if holding my orders secret. How I howled to see that. It had to be my fault, I believed then, for I had wished it dead.

I didn't kill the baby! Boy or girl, it fled on its own, while it still could.

"Oh, sir! I should have confessed to you sooner. But he swore he…he'd cut me if I told the truth!"

"Your wounds were too deep, Orpha. But you have told your secrets now and it will bring you some relief."

Beneath my ribs, my lungs open wide as wings.

·· • ··

The Woman in White is performed that weekend. Wilkie Collins's eyes light up when I rehearse, surprised I have memorized my speech after reading it twice. He gives me a speaking part, the ghostly woman herself, and a wondrous costume too: a high-waisted dress, flowing skirt, and woven cape, all of thin white gauze so that I float ghostlike across the room, lost and tragic. It's a trick, you see, hiding behind a voice and a disguise, a way of becoming someone else and disappearing. It fills my mind so full and bright that I forget everything that has happened to me. For a time.

When I take my bows, Miss Coutts, in an ivory gown with tiny pearls sewn all over it, is the first to give me a standing ovation, her shining oval face wondrous to see in the small audience. The others all follow her lead, Plorn standing upon his chair, clapping the loudest.

DICKENS'S CASE BOOK: NUMBER 98

Dare we say the words Rape or Incest in our society? Never! Yet it happens behind too many a closed door.

The cries of such abused girls rival the fierce cutting screams of the steam engine's whistle. Yet still, no one hears. Who will tell of such girls? The Haunting they endure. The girl's story is a weight that could sink one to the bottom of the Thames.

CD

That Saturday, Miss Coutts is waiting for me in Urania's parlor in pale pink and gray woolens. Her outfit is so soft and warm it's impossible to believe it's winter. Clothes have power. To disguise, surprise, and project.

"What a performance at Mr. Dickens's!" she congratulates me. "You outshone them all. You seemed…

reborn. Everyone agreed how convincing you were, as if you truly inhabited the ghost character. I was completely in awe of you. How did you do it?"

"Mr. Collins wrote the part so clearly, I just followed his directions."

"Nonsense. As a writer, he still has a great deal to learn. He is not our Mr. Dickens. He admits himself that the play needs some reworking. It was *your* voice, your bearing and costume that brought it to life. Mr. Collins even called you a muse, saying your acting inspired him to think more deeply of his character."

My whole body flushes to hear that.

"I know you love the theater as I do. How wonderful that you were brought up in one and received some training. Do you miss it?"

"I once belonged there and thought to stay forever. But—"

"Dear girl, the theater is part of you. It's there in your love of words, the way you read a book or script aloud. Your sensitivity. No one can take that away from you. People, yes." She sighs. "They come and go. It's them we miss. Tell me again of your friend in the theater. Do you still think of her?"

"Emma! When I thought of her at Tothill, it hurt like a wound."

She tilts her head. "And now?"

"I will always miss her. And wonder if she—"

"Have you tried to contact her?"

I shake my head.

"Think about it, won't you? Ivy's done you so much good. Emma could too."

Then she hands me a parcel with an expectant look. "Open it!"

Robinson Crusoe! How can she know of that day when they tugged this book out of my hands?

"You mentioned you never finished it." She smiles shyly. "It's very good writing. What a journey he took. Transporting!"

How long ago I must have told her. How carefully she listens. And remembers even the smallest of things.

·· ● ··

I fly out to the chicken shed after Miss Coutts leaves, sending Richard the Third leaping into the air.

Emma's letter is shredded and so faded now, its words are no longer legible. I know them by heart. My fingers trace the blurred lines.

Tell me the truth and I will come.

I never wanted to tell her. But just now, passing my reflection in the window, I gasp. From my hair bun to my smart boots, I look respectable. The sky-blue dress reminds me of what Ivy saw: my innocence. It's the kind of afternoon, gray and quiet, that bids me to curl up in a corner. The words arrive whole.

Dearest Emma,

Do not think I have forgotten you. It's only that I could not admit to you that I was at Tothill.

You were looking for me then. I wonder if you still are. If so, please write back to this address in Shepherd's Bush. My new home is called Urania. You would be amazed by it. And by the story I need to tell you.

Your old chum,
Orpha

Mr. Dickens arrives that day with deep circles beneath his eyes. Breathless he is, just walking across the room. That scent of violets makes me gag.

"Sir, I've been writing about the girls at Tothill. To know their story, as you do ours. Sometimes, I hear them speaking to me and then I write down what they say."

He holds my gaze with bright eyes.

"That's a good start. Even better is that you have spoken your own story aloud. Have you told another soul of it besides me?"

"Only Ivy."

He nods. "A friend to trust. How did you feel afterward?"

"We both cried, sir. It felt so natural and healing."

"It's essential to release our pain."

"Is that why you write, sir?"

"You've always been curious how I create my novels. Perhaps I should share my novelist's secrets with you now." His head tilts to the side. "Most likely. Most probably. Yes, certainly. Impressions of a lifetime are dropped into my pages. I've borrowed, begged, and stolen material from everyone I've met. But most of all, I've concealed my own self deeply inside them like a bug in amber."

That makes me gasp. "What book would I find you in, sir?"

"All! None! I have never written directly about myself. Yet you will find me in every line and every word—with every secret I've kept my whole life, even from family and friends. Between the pages of my novels are the best possible hideaways for their safekeeping."

"How do you write of yourself then?"

"Whomever I write of—David Copperfield or Oliver—becomes a vehicle. A metaphor. I write about myself *through* them, as if I were another person. A character. That gives me freedom to spill my secret pain. It's like hiding behind a mask. Surely, as an actress, you should understand that."

"Indeed. When I act, I can pretend to be most anything I am not—the Woman in White; Ophelia; Hamlet.

None of them is really me, yet somehow when I speak through them, I am more myself than ever."

"That is exactly what I do when I write." Mr. Dickens nods. "Plant in my character's heart and mind whatever I need to confess. Not that I plan it. It often leaps into the words without my say. That's my method."

He starts pacing, hands behind him. The back of his jacket is deeply wrinkled, as if he has slept in it.

"There is so much more I wanted to share with you. But we . . . might not have much more time to do so." His hand flies to his chest. "My own ghosts have been chasing me my entire life. I never rid myself of them. But you have the chance to face yours now, Orpha, and be free of Luther forever."

He says he has a proposal for me.

"Sir, I would do anything to be rid of him. Tell me how."

"Luther still lingers inside you. I sense him there. You might write of him in a personal journal. As a way to release him. To transfer him out of your heart and soul. Writing is my salvation. It could be yours too."

Shivers run through me. The rookery looms: its dead-end rattraps of alleyways. *Luther will know!*

"Orpha, make a clean sweep of it. As I never did. Never told my mother how betrayed I felt by her. It haunts me still that I never spoke up—to her or anyone. She died without knowing. And it has *never* left me."

He continues speaking in a monologue, looking out the window, as if I am not there.

"The novel I'm writing now is about political upset. Yet it yanks out of me exactly what I endure at this very moment—a situation that divides, changes everything, speaks about love, upheaval, betrayal, and all I cannot ever reveal except through it! Dare I write it?"

He whirls around to face me, coattails flying. His eyes look swollen and red. I am afraid for him.

"Yes, sir, if you can, if…if it doesn't make you ill. It sounds rather exciting. Shall I read it someday?"

"Certainly, I *must* write it. It's called *A Tale of Two Cities*. For that is exactly where I live now. Everywhere and nowhere." He points at me then. "You will do better than me. You are ready to write directly of your pain. You could be free as I *never* am. Or will be."

He will give me time to think about it, he says, for he leaves on tour again tomorrow. Then he rushes out with his papers. All I can do is plop down in a chair and try to breathe.

He gives a great gift: the secrets of his writing. Why now?

•• • ••

Ivy rushes to find me after her interview with Mr. Dickens later that month, feet flying so fast across the polished floor, she almost trips. She waves her first love letter to Jack, two pages of scribbled print.

"Dickens found Jack! In Tasmania!"

My friend spins in circles and pulls me around with her.

"He's writing Jack to tell him to save for our marriage. He's apprenticed himself to a gold prospector. Such a perfect job for him! A decent trade. Finally! The two of us will go to Tasmania in late spring to meet up with him. All of us will have a home together."

I don't tell her what I've heard about Tasmania: a wild place swarming with gold diggers, convicts, drunks, and tigers. What Ivy wants, she gets, without ever thinking ahead, like the wardrobe she bought by counterfeiting. I would never dare take such chances. I worry about the price to pay, but she never does.

Ivy can count large sums in her head and plow through a novel without letting the hard words stall her. Surely she will know what to do now. So I tell her what just happened at Tothill and Tavistock House.

Her eyes expand. "You *saw* Luther, Orpha? How terrible! You must try and get him out of your thoughts. Dickens will help you. I will too. I'm so glad you finally confessed to him. Think how free you will be once we go to Tasmania. I can't wait to get there."

She stretches out in her bed, lifting her bare toes up

in the air. "I'd give anything for Jack's kisses right now. Like a drug, kisses make me forget everything."

"Anyone's kisses?"

"Only Jack's." She looks straight at me. "You've never been kissed before? I mean...by someone who loves you?"

I lower my eyes. The bristle of his unshaven beard. His tongue licking the edges of my frozen lips. A serpent's bite.

"Oh, I'm sorry, dearest Orpha, how thoughtless of me." She touches my cheek softly. "Here I'm going on and on and forgetting that you—"

"Never mind. Tell me more. Tell me what a kiss is like."

She gasps. "Why, it's...sunlight shining only on you. Him pouring all his attention into you. You taking it in...like nectar!"

"Did you ever...lie with him?"

She nods. "I didn't just give him my body. I gave my soul."

She doesn't want it back as I do mine. Mine wasn't given. It was taken. Locked tight in the rookery. All I've ever wanted was the return of my soul.

·· ● ··

Mr. Dickens's suggestion scurries around in my head like a rat clawing underneath the floorboards. I just can't write about Luther boldly on paper. To even mention his name might conjure him.

Luther's tricky. He could get tired of waiting and make inquiries at Tothill. He might hear I'm out now and plot ways to trap me there again. He means to silence me for the stories I hold, secrets buried deep in my belly.

At any time, he could show up at Urania!

In the middle of the night, I part the curtains to check the empty street leading to London. I must be on the lookout. He could be anywhere.

·· SEVENTEEN ··

At dinner, Martha, the new resident, a girl of thirteen, straight from St. Pancras workhouse, shows up. All
morning, we heard her screaming in the back kitchen
while Miss Jane trimmed her hair to the scalp, for it was
crawling with bugs, then rubbed it with kerosene. The
odor of fuel now penetrates the room.

Martha slides next to Ivy at the table like a drowned
river rat, her hair damp and flattened. Her shoulders curl
in as if she's afraid of being hit at any moment. Sitting
beside Martha, Ivy sparkles, her dark curls bouncing and
her cheeks flushing as she tastes leftover Christmas pudding. In just four months, Ivy has changed.

"Mmm! Orange peel! Plum! Brandy!" Ivy chews,
rolling her eyes. "Nutmeg! Suet too! But what's that
heating my mouth so?"

"Ginger!" Hannah shouts. "It's my secret ingredient."

"I must learn to make such a pudding." Ivy laughs.
"My Jack will love it!"

Martha can't stop staring at Ivy. Neither can I. The
seams of Ivy's dress have been taken in by Alice to fit
her small waist. I am reminded of red poppies startling

the early spring garden in the midst of all that dead, dull brown. One can almost hear the roar of blood rushing through Ivy's veins.

Martha points to Ivy as she asks us, "Being here turns you into a lady?"

We all belly-laugh until it hurts.

"Sooner or later!" Ivy shouts. "In spite of ourselves."

·· ● ··

"Guess what's happened?" Ivy links her arm in mine after our meal, leading me near the bookshelves where we are alone.

"Dickens has written me! He's found me a position for now at the inn here in Shepherd's Bush on Saturdays when there's weddings and feasts. I'll be a serving girl there. Don't you know what this means, Orpha? I'll make money for our trip! I'll step into the world on my own! People will think me just a normal girl!"

I clap my hands. "Fanny will be so jealous!"

"Dickens says he trusts me to go out and come back on my own—which he can't do with Fanny. He thinks I might get too restless at Urania like Sesina and the others who bolted. 'It's time to change the rules,' *he* confessed to me, 'and give you girls more freedom!'"

Three and a half years she was bound in prison, longer than me. Toward the end of her sentence, she could barely lift her head. No one would ever guess it now.

On Sunday, Ivy tosses her earned coins up in the air like a juggler. She spins on the heels of her boots and laughs out loud about the gold earrings she will buy in Tasmania.

·· ● ··

Today Hannah leaves for Australia dressed in a gray woolen traveling suit we all helped to sew. I will never forget her face, ruddy and plump, blue eyes clear as spring sky, heading toward her carriage. Fanny and Leah link arms and wave goodbye. They're the next ones to emigrate, then Ivy and I.

In the back of the parlor, Alice collapses into a chair. She was supposed to leave with Hannah today. Miss Jane sets a hand on her shoulder and bends down to whisper something. Alice sighs. Gently, Miss Jane leads her up the stairs to her room, Alice leaning on her the whole way.

·· ● ··

Ivy finds me writing in the garden and sits down beside me on the bench.

"Fanny and Leah tease one another that they are twins, going off to Australia together. You and I are sisters. Not twins."

"What do you mean, Ivy?"

"We tell each other everything. Like bosom friends and sisters do. But you and I differ. I love the bustle of the inn and the streets but you don't. You need quiet and all those books in the library."

I nod. "That's how I've always been. It's such a comfort to find them at Urania. That's what Mr. Dickens offered me, just like he arranged for you to work at the inn. He knows us well."

"I know more about you than you think. You write. I hear your quill scratching even in the middle of the night. But you never tell me what you write about. Will you?"

She points to the papers piled on my lap.

I hold my breath. She's never asked before.

"Is it private?"

I shake my head. It's been contained inside me all this time like a secret hive. Only I could hear it buzzing. Only I could believe that somewhere out of sight, hidden in the chicken shed or in the dead of night, honey spilled over. "Your wounds were too deep," Mr. Dickens said.

"So, who's it about?" Ivy persists.

"Girls like us, the ones at Tothill, who were so lost. I want to tell it so people know how prison made girls suffer so much for such small acts that they were forever ruined."

I hand the pages over.

Ivy shakes her head. "I can't follow script yet. Read it to me!"

I remember Pa facing his audiences, how he could

capture all their attention with just one sentence spoken, solemn and resonating across the dark. So I read aloud while Ivy shuts her eyes. When I finish, she sits straight up, her eyes brightening.

"All the while you read, I could see it right in front of me: the prison corridors, its narrow cells, the girls trapped inside. And their voices so heartbreaking! However did you find out their real stories?"

I could feel my face flushing. "Some was told to me in a few whispered words. Some was what I felt deep inside. Glimpses down dark hallways. Hunches and guesses. Watching how a girl moved to tell me all about her."

"It's like a book!" Ivy jumps to her feet. "I can *see* it! Girls move in scenes from cell to oakum room to chapel. I was there, Orpha! This is about all of us at Tothill. And it's real. A true story!"

I am spellbound.

My mind separates from the rest of me, lifts high above, and spins. I look far down at the broken girl below who once was *me*. How could she have written a book?

She was no one: a girl in pieces. Her soul stolen. Who wrote it, then?

Me! It was a slice of my own soul flying back.

"*We* have secured posts for you and Ivy." Miss Coutts calls us both into the parlor one morning. "Ivy shall be a maid in an inn until she marries. And Orpha will be governess to the children of the Governor of Tasmania!"

"Oh!" screams Ivy, jumping up. "When do we sail?"

"April. You should be able to write as well as you read by then."

Words leap out of me. "It's too soon! I'm not ready!"

Must I go? Couldn't I stay in England? Or remain at Urania?

Ivy gasps, turning to me, as if hearing my thoughts.

Miss Coutts shakes her head. "My dear Orpha, how many times have I heard those words, even from girls who couldn't wait to emigrate! When it came time to leave, they all confessed how afraid they were. That's quite to be expected. It's just nerves, dear girl."

Ivy frowns at me, leaning closer to our benefactor. "You know she's been writing? Lots! A book! Has she said?"

"I knew about the ink. Nothing more." The lady turns to me, her eyes widening. "Can you show it to me? I would be very interested in it."

"See?" Ivy nudges me. "She's curious, just as I was. Orpha wrote it true, miss, about that awful place whose name we cannot say aloud."

I run to the shed, carrying the pages back, loose and trembling in my hands like fragile eggs. They are the dark secrets that spilled into my blood, veins, and arteries. I pass them to Miss Coutts with fumbling hands, pages spilling everywhere.

On the way out of the room, Ivy links her arm in mine.

"You *told* her!" I hiss at her.

"I had to. She must know all about you. Dickens doesn't come around much anymore. Besides, she owns this place. She's the one really in charge. Who's to tell her if I don't? Who's to help you if she doesn't?"

Winter shivers through me. Without my pages, I feel naked.

·· ● ··

A whole month passes without a visit or even a letter from Mr. Dickens. I keep glancing out the front window, holding vigil. Often, I walk out to the front gate, listening for the afternoon train from London. In the evenings, knitting with the others, I listen for him coming in the door, swinging his walking stick, tipping his top hat to us: "Good evening, girls!"

But there is no sign of Mr. Dickens.

One morning, a telegram arrives that Mrs. Marchmont tears open, reads through twice, and hastily stuffs into her pocket. Her whole body sags afterward. Suddenly, she looks years older. She turns toward London, her lips pressing into a tight line as if she's swallowed bitterness itself.

Gathering my cleaning rags, I head to the back parlor, shutting the door behind me. If the room shines, surely he will return. Layers of dust cover all the furniture. The desk is piled with letters and books, the quills neatly arranged, and there is ink in the bottle.

Suddenly I see what's missing.

The shelf in the glass cabinet is empty. I rattle its door. *Locked!* The Case Book is gone. My story too.

Greedily, I yank open the desk drawers and check. They are all empty. Not one paper is left. The key is not there. Everything has vanished with Mr. Dickens.

·· ▪ ··

That very afternoon, Miss Coutts arrives, although it is not a Saturday. She bustles straight to the kitchen, where the matron is giving cooking lessons. Pots immediately clang to the floor.

"I'm all butter fingers!" cries Martha.

She and Ivy are ordered out of the kitchen at once, still in aprons.

Through the kitchen door travel the loud voices of Miss Coutts and the matron. We three press in.

"How can anyone do such a thing!"

"Mr. Dickens dares to."

Miss Coutts lowers her voice. We lean closer. "Her name is Nelly, an actress he met in August, of the Ternan acting family. She was only eighteen when he met her last fall."

"Oh! What will happen to his family? To Mrs. Dickens?"

"Catherine will leave Tavistock at once. Such a disgrace for the poor woman. She was my friend, as was Charles. And we both know quite well that he, with his own name to protect, cannot divorce or ever marry this girl or bring her into society. So why do it?"

A gasp from the matron. "Then she will be his... mistress!"

"Charles has done the unthinkable—what men do. He was my partner in many a project, but he will no longer be part of Urania. So we, as women, must carry on and guide our girls. Without him."

Ivy's mouth falls open and she reaches out to steady herself against me. I never told her how I felt him slipping away after I had read the secrets in his journal. It began with the scent of violets that September day, an intoxicating smell that made him dream his own soul away.

I remember the last thing he said to me about writing

A Tale of Two Cities. The man is divided; he lives in both those cities. From now on, he'll roam lost between the two of them.

·· ● ··

Miss Coutts calls for me within the hour. I find her sitting at Mr. Dickens's desk, clenching his quill tightly, her mouth in a flat line. She straightens when she sees me, her eyes dark and penetrating. Gone is her soft smile.

"I will be your advisor from now on instead of Mr. Dickens. Of course, you can meet with Mr. Chesterson anytime. Especially as we help prepare you for your journey. I believe that there is something still to be done for you. Mr. Dickens has informed me of the progress of all our girls—Ivy's success at the inn and your progress in writing lessons. All our girls' lives and hardships, he has told me. Including yours."

I sit still and wait.

"I have heard stories like yours, Orpha, from too many a girl. Secrets held between them, Mr. Dickens, and myself. Stories confessed by weeping girls to my pastor. Indeed, I have to look no farther than my own stoop to see fallen girls preyed upon by men. Yet these problems have largely been ignored by those in charge."

She hands over my pages, neatly tied with a green ribbon.

"Your manuscript pierces the truth. It is heartbreaking. Well written. Imagistic. Haunting. I visited Tothill when I first imagined Urania. What a shock it was! Girls and boys tossed away like rubbish. Broken and hardened because of what was done to them. Your words bring it to life as no report I've read. You have achieved something startling. Except for one thing."

She halts. "You didn't tell what happened to *you*. That's the most important part. That you must write too."

"I don't know how, miss."

I don't say what Mr. Dickens advised—to write directly of Luther.

She leans forward. "Read your work again. You will be surprised how clear it is. See yourself as one of the girls at Tothill. Bit by bit, slip yourself into what is already written. Rewrite it on fresh pages."

She hands me a gift then: a leather-bound lady's journal with flowers engraved in blue and gold paint on the cover. Inside are thick pages, white and untouched, too many to count.

"I painted those flowers myself. And thought how practical it could be to contain all your thoughts in one place without pages falling everywhere. Will you use it?"

I am already hugging the journal to my chest. This woman knows me better than anyone. She's guessed what I've been longing for: words and white space to hold them in. My smile must reach my ears. *If only I could do as she asks!*

····•····

The new journal sits on my desk. Its creamy pages are too clean to disturb with what I have to say; its cover too smooth to mar. I turn images over and over in my mind like a Chinese puzzle box but meet only dead ends. The story can't find an opening. In the middle of the night, awakening from dreams of a man in a darkened doorway, I cannot fall back asleep for hours.

"Every alley and every drainpipe leading to the sewers, I've crept through all their twists and turns," I hear Luther warn. *"Every alcove up and down the lanes, I know like the back of my hand. I'll dig you out."*

····•····

Another new girl arrives, Kate, leaning on the matron as if she has difficulty standing. She has deep purple bags beneath her eyes, wispy hair, and a waist hollowed out as if she has never eaten her fill.

"A child's dress could fit her!" Alice mumbles upon seeing her, cutting one of our old dresses down.

Mrs. Marchmont pulls Ivy and me aside. "Kate's come from an asylum, where she's been resting after a stay at Tothill. Be kind to her. She needs to build her strength."

"I swallowed essential oil of almonds this last time," Kate admits when we girls are alone with her. "Found me passed out on a park bench and sent me to prison for harming myself, after a hospital stay."

"Why would you ever do that?" Ivy asks. "That could kill you!"

"I had no one left who cared. I didn't matter to anyone. Mr. Dickens heard of me and got me to an asylum. Then here."

Ivy and I exchange a dark look. Without a word, we seat her between us at dinner, heaping her plate full. Kate won't have Mr. Dickens to guide her now. Mr. Chesterson comes to interview her instead. He's a solid wall. Mr. Dickens was sky.

·· • ··

Day after day passes and I can't sit still long. I jump up and run outside in my free time to pace the whole yard, between the sleeping garden beds, around and around the chicken shed.

Who said, "All the world's a stage, and all the men and women merely players; they have their exits and their entrances, and one man in his time plays many parts"? Shakespeare! For me, this world is a labyrinth. And I am lost without an exit.

The next day, it's the same: up and down the stairs, always in motion; determined to start writing that afternoon; unable to sit down. Mr. Dickens told me he would "go down a railroad," walk a dozen miles, or roam the midnight streets when such a mood was upon him.

Yet he went on to write all those books.

How's it done?

I wove my first stories like a spider spinning its web. Without thinking. Only knowing and listening.

Now I remember Mr. Dickens saying he wrote of himself as if watching another character. At Tothill, the pain was so numbing, the cell they bound me inside so stifling, I did think of myself as another person. Otherwise, I might not have endured.

I've done it before in my own way.

When will the words throb again, beating like drums, vibrating like lutes, announcing their arrival? They must make me come to them.

·· ● ··

It's the evening the girls are officially told that Mr. Dickens has gone for good. Martha hasn't even met him. Yet she hisses in my ears, "We got to act like virgins and that Dickens does what he wants! That's a man for you!"

Leah has just finished sewing the last stitch on her traveling suit, holding it high for us to admire. She drops it to the floor with a gasp.

"He left?" shouts Kate. "And never said goodbye?"

Alice shakes her head and sighs. "He won't see me emigrate now. And that's what he said he hoped for."

As the girls leave, Mrs. Marchmont asks me to stay behind.

"You will go on without him, Orpha. As I did when my own husband died. For a time, everything died with him. Bit by bit, as I grew into widowhood, I found the strength I never knew I had."

"I still need his help," I tell her, head down.

Her hand rests heavily on my shoulder.

"Many a girl leaves Urania and I worry about her as if she were my own daughter. Some leave without maturing—Jemima, Sesina. But you have blossomed here. Wherever you go, you will do well.

"Orpha," she continues. "You will be very busy sewing your traveling suit and finishing a new summer shawl for Tasmania. And you are also working on a project for Miss Coutts. Is that not so?"

"Yes, she suggested…if I can…that I should write what made me fall. A story of how a man can ruin a girl."

"Then you must do it without fail. You don't have much time left with us. I can release you from kitchen duties and Saturday cleaning. We have new recruits here who will do it instead. Will this give you the time you need for your project?"

For answer, I stand and curtsy quite low as if she were

a queen and I her subject, given a royal gift. She smiles at that.

·· ● ··

The nightmare returns. I am flying through the London night, dark passages wherever I turn. Creeping along a gangplank above the stage, eyes straight ahead on Emma at her perch across the open air. She reaches her hands to me across the great abyss below that is the stage. Crawling…balancing…then suddenly, my nightgown is yanked and there's a pressing weight pinning me down in my cot. One hand presses my lips shut and the other is ripping my bare legs apart.

I awaken the whole house with my screaming.

·· ● ··

Early the next morning Miss Jane pulls me aside, into the back parlor, to ask about it.

"I dreamed about…my past. It haunts me still."

"Perhaps it's time to let what happened go somewhere it can't harm you anymore."

"Where? It's part of me. It's my story!"

"When I was younger, I was overwhelmed, much as you are now. Behind me was a sad story: the story of my limp, what set me apart. If I had dwelt on that story, I wouldn't be here with you right now. I had to let it go. And become someone new. As you must too."

She studies my face, my hands clenching and

unclenching, even my dress put on that day all crooked and wrinkled. She smooths my collar flat and straightens my hem.

Then she says, "Do what you know you must do in your own heart. What you crave to do. What you deeply desire. Be who you were meant to be and more! Even if you are afraid!"

"Tell me it's possible!" I cry.

"More than possible, Orpha. I have done so myself. And so has many a girl who has passed through Urania. Hannah, Leah, and Ivy are doing so. You will too."

·· ● ··

Fanny hugs everyone early one morning, dancing out the door. She didn't stop chattering a single moment all this week, preparing for the journey. Now she boards the carriage outside, waving wildly to us.

Leah clings to me in the front yard. "My story is safe with you now. I will never forget that. No one in Australia will ever know it. Unless I choose to tell it. And I won't. It's between us."

With that, she rushes into the carriage and is pulled away. Without their bright voices and laughter, their skirts swinging through the rooms, Urania echoes.

You only notice the emptiness when someone's gone for good.

·· ● ··

Ivy finds me lying on my bed in the early evening instead of joining the other girls in the parlor.

"You've stopped writing. All you do is doodle and dream. And you're not helping get ready for our journey. My new suit needs hemming and my shawl will never get done if you don't finish crocheting the edges. Stop looking out the window for Dickens to come back!"

"What good does it do to write? Emma hasn't answered. I've lost her too, just like Mr. Dickens and Pa."

"Finish your story!" Ivy shouts at me. "Just tell it and get it out. That man deserves to be condemned for what he did to you!"

"Luther is dangerous, Ivy. You don't know what he's like. He could find me yet."

·· ● ··

Miss Coutts calls for me after her interview with Ivy. As Ivy leaves the parlor, she dangles a blue-glass-beaded purse from her arm, a going-away gift from our benefactor. Ivy is glowing.

She squeezes my hand. "She's got a plan for you. Do as she asks."

Miss Coutts looks up from her notes. "I wish to speak to you about something I want you to do."

We sit face-to-face just as Mr. Dickens and I used to do.

"I believe there must now be a reckoning. A telling.

From someone as wronged as you have been, imprisoned by another's crime. There has never been a girl like you before. One who observes closely and knows how to aim her words with fire and precision."

She leans forward and places her slender hand on mine. Her eyes and lips soften and she is the Miss Coutts I know.

"You have a month and a half before you sail. And sail you must or you will never escape the fear of that man finding you. Before you go, leave this tale behind you forever. Write your own story, Orpha. Do it for yourself and all the other girls just like you—unprotected girls who suffer abuse. And if you do so, I will publish it for all of London to read."

This knocks the breath out of me.

"I have tried...but so far, it escapes me. It's too hard to do."

"Just because something is difficult does not mean it's impossible. You *have* been writing. Your manuscript is stunning so far. You have had an apprenticeship with the greatest writer of our time. That means you are ready to write of yourself and what pushed you into Tothill."

"Do you really mean to publish it?"

"Yes. I have the means to do so. I'd go straight to the same press Mr. Dickens uses, so it will look professional.

It cannot have your name printed on the pamphlet, of course. That would be too risky."

"If I write the truth, shouldn't I use my own name?"

Slowly she shakes her head. "I wish it could be done. But not in our times. There are ways around it, though. When Charlotte Brontë was ready to publish and was told that 'literature cannot be the business of a woman's life,' she did what other women do. Found a pen name. A pseudonym. As George Sand did. And our Mr. Dickens too."

"If I . . . write it, am I free to decide what to do with it?"

"Of course. It's your story, after all. But this city needs to hear it. For once it has been told, London will be shocked to hear what can happen to innocent girls. Many will be moved to save them. I'd like to distribute copies to top members of Parliament and society, influential men. And their wives too, who won't ever stop nagging until their husbands do something. You shall have the rest of the pamphlets. Do you agree?"

She must see my ear-to-ear smile. She claps her hands together in triumph.

"You will succeed, dear Orpha. I know it. Your own words will do more good to help girls at risk than any charity I donate to."

·· ● ··

I run to Ivy at once to tell her.

But she speaks first. "Once it's published, you'll be gone from this country, Orpha. That man won't be able to touch you. She said you needed a false name. Pick one. And get down to work!"

My mouth drops open. She already knows what Miss Coutts proposed.

"You must want this so much, you'll never stop until you've done it," Ivy says. "I've been trying to teach you that."

There's a look I never saw on her face before: sharp and cunning, her eyes cutting. I wonder what she has been saying to Miss Coutts.

"Once I have my mind set, I go after what I want. Jack taught me that. 'If you can't get in by the front door,' he always said, 'you'll have to sneak in through the back door!' You're my closest chum. I'd do anything for you. But I can't write. And I can't take up the lady's offer. That you must do on your own. And you will! I'll help you too, do some of your work to free your time."

She takes my hands and spins me around in circles, making me dizzy, her voice breathless.

"Look how it's turned out, Orpha! Jack would… never…ever have done good in London. You knew that, didn't you? But he has no choice now. It's all been arranged. The three of us will be a family, like I wished for. It'll make up for the ones we lost."

Her head tips back as she heaves big gulps of laughter from her belly.

Suddenly, she's the girl she must have been once, well before Tothill, long before Jack. I lean way back, letting her arms take my weight, and twirl with her, my bosom friend, to someplace light and free I have not been in many years: *girlhood!*

Miss Coutts has promised me!

·· • ··

The words need conjuring. They are drumming. They are piping. But they can't push past…

Never did I feel that I was good enough.

At nine, wishing to call Pa back from the drink.

At thirteen, unable to fend Luther off.

At seventeen, yearning for Mr. Dickens to see me emigrate.

Mr. Dickens abandons me. Just as they all did.

For a man's treasures: a young woman; gin; pleasures all his own. Without a thought for the unfinished girl left behind.

Just like Luther! Just like Pa!

One betrayed my body. One betrayed my heart. All betrayed my soul.

I am fallen because of a man. And that story is hidden within cobwebs and dust and silence.

Where is that girl Orpha, hidden behind her costume and

disguise? The child who could play and sing, the one who play-acted in the dark, pretending to be anyone she wished to be. The one who flung herself to unknown places.

And then my whole chest opens wide. *She's right here!*

Mr. Dickens carries me in the Case Book. Wherever he goes, my story goes with him. But that story is *not* his! It's *mine! I want it back!* "Society will never accept writing from a fallen girl. That would be scandalous!" he told me. "One needs a name, family, money. And a husband too."

I will do this without him. Without any of *his* requirements. And I shall claim better: a circle of women, my own story, and a new name.

•• ● ••

That night I stay awake and reread my manuscript. It sweeps me back into Tothill upon the wave of words.

When I put it down, my whole body trembles. I've almost done it! The skeleton is there: the setting; the atmosphere; the girls I knew. What's missing is myself and the time before Tothill; Pa and the workhouse; owned body and soul by Uncle Luther; the brothel; the hard fall in the street; and the hospital.

"Later," Mr. Dickens advised. "Later, you can build a story on the skeleton of those few jottings."

I know what it is now. It was always Orpha's story. But it's bigger than just mine. It's the story of every fallen girl everywhere.

Before dawn, I write alone, fiercely scratching my quill inside the creamy pages of the journal as if the paper were oakum to pierce. I tell of my childhood. It churns like butter. Then I dip dark black ink and scrape new lines onto the margins of the old draft about spiraling down toward Tothill, then the isolation of that prison.

Ivy delivers meals to my desk. Not a word do I say aloud to her.

My quill leaks and sparks, opens wide the wounds of those nights. Between the pages, my blue baby falls to the ground. Luther's grunts and the sloshing of gin down his throat fill this very room. Then the stink of sewer and river-deep mud drifts past my nose.

He's come! Conjured. *Here!*

I don't flinch. Or step back. Or hesitate. This time, there's a weapon in my hands: the truth etched in dark black ink, words for the telling.

Words can chiv too. They can name; they can carve out the wound, and slice the abuser wide open.

"Be bricky, Orpha!" Ivy calls over to me later from the dark side of our room as I write through the night in the moonlight by the window.

I tell Luther all.

"*There's* someone here to see you!" Miss Jane, her face flushed, rushes into the yard to find me. "Name of Mrs. Clark, Mrs. Emma Clark. Says she received a letter from you and…"

My feet run before I hear the rest.

Emma's dress likely was once blue but is sun-faded now, rimmed with street dirt all along the hem. Above it, her face is dazzling bright, curls falling out of her bonnet just as I remember.

"Well now, shall I curtsy to your ladyship?" Her glance sweeps over me as she grins.

With that, I run toward her and we hug for a long while, each of us shedding tears. When I step away, my hand touches a head below my knee.

"Who's this?"

A child hides behind Emma, clinging to her skirts.

"This is my little girl, almost two. We call her Orpha. I am married to a good man, Henry, on his way up. He's clerk to a lawyer. Pa loves him as much as we do."

The girl peeks out at me, her curls matching her mother's. Then she disappears, giggling.

"Well, little Orpha," says Emma. "Aren't you going to give it to her?"

The child peeks out again and hands me a package wrapped in twine.

"Go ahead, open it."

Sequins spill out of the package like stars in a sky of twilight. My mother's dress!

"Happy eighteenth birthday, dear Orpha! I've waited all these years to give you this present, hoping you'd come back. Pa and I saved it for you."

I press the dress against me. The theater is embedded in it: old wood, musty curtains, and my mother's voice commanding lutes and drums.

All I can do is hug her again. "I have...so much to tell you, Emma."

"You don't have to tell me anything. Someone wronged you. Grievously. I felt it like a knife to my heart when I heard about Tothill. Finally got up the courage to go there. And they said you were gone. Wouldn't tell me where. Not until the letters did I know how to find you."

"*Letters?*"

"First Miss Coutts, telling me you were safe and that you would write once you were healed. Then yours came."

I do tell her everything then, pulling her into a chair

next to me with the child on her lap, sucking her thumb and soon falling asleep. I feel like Robinson Crusoe, lost at sea all these years, finally returning home to her.

"We never should have let you go from the theater that day." She sighs.

"You had no choice," I assure her. "I had to pay Pa's debt. You couldn't have stopped them."

She stares at me darkly. "When we looked for you last Christmas at your aunt's, Luther stood there, curses spitting from his mouth. Soon as I saw him, I got the shivers. It was then I guessed."

"Well, I'm freeing myself of that man—wait till I tell you how! You won't believe my plan! And look how we found one another at last."

I remember the two of us playing in the theater. Her daring. Her hands across the gangplank, grabbing me to safety over the abyss. It's Emma's hands I need now. I grab them tightly in my own and tell her what needs to be done.

Before she leaves, she makes a promise.

"Yes!" Her eyes light up. "I'll do my part. You do yours. Together, we'll take our revenge!"

"What a great thump we will make!" I shout.

We bend over, belly-laughing, as if not even a day had passed since we were young girls together.

·· ● ··

"Come down, Orpha!"

"Time to get fitted for your traveling dress!"

I ignore the shouts. Upstairs, I shut the door to our room and prop a chair against the doorknob. Quiet! These girls are never quiet.

I may seem to be quite ordinary, just a girl sitting in a chair staring out the window. But I am not ordinary. A scene is forming inside and I will myself to be still and listen to it speak. Set my mind loose from my body so I am free to watch as images rise. I do nothing, nothing but hold still, until the story unravels. Then I rush to write it down without speaking or even thinking. If I don't do this at once, it's gone, like a flame in the wind.

The words from the old draft have been copied into the journal along with bits and pieces of my own story. Beneath my hands it speaks, cutting and raw. The voices are clear as Westminster bells clanging in the rookery, tolling their names one by one: Rose, Edwina, Hester, E25, "the suicide," A11, Ivy, Luther, and a girl named Orpha whose story is revealed. Haunting Tothill's corridors, and each and every lane of London's rookeries, rises a high wail: the voices of all the innocent babies born only to suffer and die.

Listen!

This moment roars with a thousand words and stories dancing in my head. Intoxicating!

Now I know why Mr. Dickens got so lost when he wrote, forgetting who he was and where he was.

·· ● ··

The leather journal is filled now. Miss Jane will carry it to Miss Coutts's home in Piccadilly.

"It's the quickest way," she explains. "And the safest. She promises to return it to you within two weeks. Just in time for your voyage. Along with her offer, she says."

By the window in our room, Ivy and I burst free with shouts and cheers as we watch Miss Jane below step into a waiting carriage with my manuscript in her bag. Our feet are stomping too, shaking the dresser and threatening the mirror hanging above it. In Ivy's round brown eyes, I finally see reflected the girl I once was.

I am not that girl on the cot, she who wept beside a dead father; or the one forever stuck on the gangplank. I am no longer living in those places. Those were just the things that happened to me.

·· ● ··

For the first time in a month, I step down into the parlor for supper at the table and breathe the place in. It seems I've been away for years, it looks so fresh.

Why hadn't I noticed it before: the waxed wooden floors; the shimmering emerald moiré curtains sewn by Alice; and the polished surfaces of the oak furniture? We girls have scrubbed this house spotless. All crimes have been bleached away. Urania is fit for virgins such as us.

Mrs. Marchmont pats my shoulder. "Well done, Orpha! We knew you could do it."

Alice is waiting for me, patting the seat beside her. I plop right down.

Martha grins. "Welcome back to earth! You been gone such a long time up in your room, thought you were kept a prisoner."

She jumps up and twirls for me in a lilac dress that once was Sesina's.

Kate's cheeks are pinked now and fuller. At our meal, she's already learned to take extra from Alice's plate as I used to.

"They say you can write. Can you teach me how?" she begs.

"Of course. Right after this, I'll show you how to make your letters."

These girls are my sunlit walls. Never again can thoughts of Luther sneak into these coal-warmed rooms with their robin's-egg-blue paint. It's too holy a refuge for him. We girls have fairy-ringed this home with all kinds of bloody spells.

·· TWENTY ··

The sun is piercing, the wind gale-strong and tugging at my bonnet ties, pushing me back from the railing, away from London. My bombazine dress blows too, vivid and voluminous in its skirts, its plum-and-lavender piping sharp against the dull weathered timber of the *Victoria*. In my small leather bag, purchased with Urania's wages, are tucked my engraved journal, a new quill, and ink, along with my gifts. Beside me, Ivy in her vivid yellow dress, her face rosy, shouts and waves furiously to Miss Coutts and Mrs. Marchmont, who stand on the shore, waving back.

Between England and me are water and wind.

Water widening by the second.

Wind lifting the sails away from this land to elsewhere.

I turn toward the direction of the rookery, where Emma has been sneaking through the dead of night in the company of her husband and her father, flinging my published story, wrapped in green paper, all throughout the rookery, letting it fly like paper birds. *The Girl from Tothill* unravels for all to see. At every tavern. By every corner. In every shop. Stacks on every street cart. In front of dwellings where readers live. The residents all delighted come this bright morning at the luck of awakening to a brand-new pamphlet landing on their doorsteps. Free!

All around the rookery they will stop to read, their eyes widening to hear about the girl Orpha whom a man called Mr. A. Grace tells of.

A man has revealed how fragile a girl is in our rookery, living right here among us.

And all those other lost girls who did so little wrong, who only needed a mother. Why, they are treasures, aren't they?

Doesn't the author look the gentleman? Here's his picture. Dressed as fine as Dickens. Read his outrage!

And the young girl too, the one named Orpha. Isn't she from that acting family over on Old Pye Street? She has written a letter straight to her abuser. Listen!

To Luther,

I was your twelve-year-old orphaned niece.

You betrayed me.

You were supposed to be my uncle, protector, and guardian.

Instead, you raped me. Not once. But over and over again.

I lived in fear of you and your knife.

It should have been you, Luther, damned to prison,

instead of me.
Now let the world know and condemn you as I do.
For I am free of you now and forever.
I live; I prosper; I survive.

Miss Orpha Wood

How readers will whisper the story to their neighbors who cannot read, tell the housebound, shout to the hard of hearing, visit house after house with the news, gossip in the taverns, and point out the words to anyone passing by. And then head out and gather together with that pamphlet squeezed in their hands toward Luther's dark and shuttered door on Great St. Anne's Lane. They will stop boldly there to knock and stare and shout names. There will be crowds of them. And he will hide with my aunt in the dampest, farthest corner and shrink from their sight.

All around the rookery, girls will hasten to their houses as soon as dark falls, their families looking out the window for them to come safely home. And in the fine homes of Piccadilly, and of government officials, doctors, bishops, and clergymen, friends of Miss Coutts, the well-to-do, will sink into their chairs, gasping. For they will finally understand what can happen to an unprotected girl.

• • •

In five months, we will land in Tasmania. I have already decided that I can write there, for I am told I will have a room of my own after the day's duties are done. Ivy has fussed about that. She will room at the inn with ten other serving girls. But she will have her Jack, who will come and go from the gold mines to visit her. Even when she marries, I won't be alone. If she marries. Every sailor aboard this ship has his eye on her.

Besides, you are never alone when you write and entertain your characters as if they breathed in the room right beside you.

When Mr. Dickens showed his first writing to the world, he did so with a pseudonym: Boz. It served him like a charm. Now I have one too: Mr. A. Grace! In this society, a gentleman's name opens doors.

Forever Mr. Dickens will remain part of me.

Father. Teacher. Mentor. He played all those roles.

This is what he taught me: When words fill your mind, you forget your own self; you become a higher self. A conduit. Full of something called grace. Like my own father, he planted words, tiny seeds that grew, until the words became him and he was the book. And then he fed them to me.

All you must do then is set them free.

MR. A. GRACE

·· AUTHOR'S NOTE ··

I first encountered Dickens when I was a girl living in a semirural strand of Ontario's fruit belt. He reached across the century and the ocean with satire, quirky characters, and sharp stabs at social injustice. His portrayals of unforgettable Victorian characters so awakened me to the presence of universal archetypes that I began to notice them all around me. I fell in love with Dickens's voice and his conjuring of worlds, both external and internal, and dreamed of becoming a writer.

Years later, I met him again in *Charles Dickens at 200*, a bicentennial exhibit of his life and work at the Morgan Library & Museum in New York City, amid a collection of his quills, the draft of a very worked-over *A Christmas Carol*, portraits of that famous face, and samples of his self-taught shorthand. His letters to Angela Burdett-Coutts brought me to a full stop: tongue-in-cheek stories of Urania's girls; ideas about decorating the home; a plea for vivid color in the girls' dresses; apt nicknames for them; and, of course, their antics, such as breaking into Urania's supply of beer and entertaining policemen in the middle of the night.

Dickens hoped for a magical transformation of his "virgin charges," his damaged girls. So who were these girls and where did they come from? Who succeeded and why did they do so? On my way to the New York Public Library years later to search for answers to those questions, I suddenly had an impression of an imaginary girl sitting opposite me on the train. Tiny, thin, with straight blond hair so thick it seemed like a horse's mane, she slid in like a shadow and accompanied me to the library. At that moment, I knew I would write this novel. When the main character shows up, so does his or her voice, setting the emotional tone needed to write. Later I would read how Dickens floundered, ungrounded, when entering a book, taking notes and long walks like his "benders" until his main character arrived and wouldn't stop talking.

Urania operated from 1847 to 1862. While no official record was ever located of all the girls who entered the home, usually twelve at a time, it is estimated that a hundred of Urania's girls emigrated overseas (*Charles Dickens and the House of Fallen Women*, by Jenny Hartley). Dickens's Case Book was not found either; it's speculated that it was burned with letters and other papers spanning twenty years in a bonfire Dickens set in 1860. Of this event, Dickens wrote: "They sent up a smoke like the Genie when he got out of the casket on the seashore." Most characters in this book are composites of actual girls who lived at the home. Orpha is my own creation. While I used some of the actual names of the girls, only the stories of Rhena Pollard and Alice Matthews are true. Alice died aboard ship when she finally emigrated, a common occurrence of the time because of epidemics. She took a bad turn after the equator, giving thanks to Miss Coutts. "Death held no terrors for her," wrote a passenger present at her bedside.

I am indebted to the Queens Library and the New York Public Library for providing a wide range of research materials on Dickens. For the invaluable assistance received at the Sherman Fairchild Reading Room at the Morgan Library & Museum, I am deeply grateful. The multivolumed book by Dickens's chosen biographer and personal friend, John Forster's *The Life of Charles Dickens*, was the perfect start, along with the work of Peter Ackroyd, whose *Dickens* and books about London created a vivid background, as did Robert Douglas-Fairhurst's *Becoming Dickens*. Dickens hid the truth about Ellen (Nelly) Ternan in his own lifetime, and Forster shielded him. In Claire Tomalin's *Charles Dickens: A Life* and *The Invisible Woman: The Story of Nelly Ternan and Charles Dickens*, that secret was explored. Jane Smiley's *Charles Dickens: A Life* examines his writerly life, as does *Dickens's Working Notes for his Novels*, edited by Harry Stone. The books that so immersed me in the era and street life that I could smell and taste 1850s London were Henry Mayhew's *London Labour and the London Poor* and Ruth Goodman's *How to Be a Victorian*, the latter providing fun details on grooming, dress, and lifestyle. Finally, in Dickens's own novels and letters (*Letters of Charles Dickens to the Baroness Burdett-Coutts*), I encountered the author himself. The writing of *David Copperfield* spanned the Urania years, and the novel is viewed as semiautobiographical; in it Dickens revealed the trials of his own early life through David, just as the girls had confessed to him.

Dickens abandoned Urania suddenly and without notice after a committee meeting in April 1858. While I tried to keep to his busy timeline, I have taken liberties with some of the dates to serve the story's plot. Any mistake or manipulation of that timeline is my own. Some of Dickens's comments and conversations in this novel are based on actual excerpts from his voluminous letters.

Miss Coutts, the wealthiest woman in Europe of her time, devoted so much of her fortune to charity that she was named Queen of the Poor. Her many projects included assistance for impoverished weavers to establish their trade in the colonies; free vocational training for the uneducated; training for prostitutes in needlework and cooking; redevelopment of slum areas like Bethnal Green that housed the poor; campaigns against cruelty to animals; protection for street vendors such as flower girls and fruit sellers; and medical support and food for cholera victims, to name only a few. I have kept Dr. Brown on at Urania, since he was an invaluable advisor and close friend to Miss Coutts for years. He died in 1855.

Laudanum, "black drops," an opium derivative, was in common use in the Victorian period, a kind of everyday aspirin. It was viewed as a remedy for all kinds of ills from menopause to insomnia and nervousness. Not known to be addictive at the time, it was so readily available without a prescription that it led to the first opiate epidemic in Europe. Many fell victim to it: Catherine Dickens, Charles Dickens, Wilkie Collins, and the poets Keats, Shelley, and Coleridge. By 1916, it became a controlled substance in England; it was finally banned in 1920.

Of interest to those eager to explore more about the suppression of women are novels such as Margaret Atwood's *Alias Grace* and *The Handmaid's Tale*, and Sarah Waters's *Affinity*. In film, *Albert Nobbs* and *The Invisible Woman* both explore women's plight in the Victorian era.

I hope that the spunk exhibited by Urania's girls in surviving and coming of age in a difficult era, one of haves and have-nots, thrives in today's world, a parallel universe—one of historic worldwide homelessness, poverty, and displacement, and one of dominance by the one percent. May every girl know the blessings of a mentor and the promise of second chances. May she say yes to both!

Finally, in my own life, I am grateful for the presence of mentors and the grace of second chances that opened doors, lanes, and pathways around me. This circle includes my editor, Mary Cash, for her amazing sensitivity and belief in Orpha's story, and my agent, Fiona Kenshole, who saw its potential from the earliest drafts. To my first reader always and forever, Neil Schwartz, and my intuitive circle of writers—Denise Dailey, Leslie Sharpe, Eva Hill, and Raphael Sason. For all their support, I feel blessed.

Virginia Frances Schwartz

A GLOSSARY OF VICTORIAN SLANG

Slang was the common speech among Victorian working and criminal classes. As Dickens roamed London's streets on his famous walks, he became fascinated by this colorful dialect. So did Chesterson, Coldbaths's governor, who called it "flash language." Dickens incorporated many slang words, derivatives of Old English, into his novels. By writing slang down for the first time in a novel, Charles Dickens caused it to reach a wider audience and helped transform slang words into acceptable and commonly used words.

*Words and phrases marked with an asterisk were found in the *Oxford English Dictionary*.

*abuzz: buzzing with excessive gossip or activity

arse: British spelling of *ass*

bah humbug!: a dismissal of something commonly liked; an expression made famous by Dickens's character Ebenezer Scrooge

bang-up: very fine

*batty: crazy

batty-fang: to smash up

*blast: a word used to express annoyance

*bosom friend: best friend

bricky: brave

*butter fingers: careless

chiv: to cut or stab

chum: friend

church bell: a talkative woman

coiner: a coin counterfeiter

collie shangles: a quarrel

*comfoozled: exhausted

*dandy: a man unduly devoted to style and dress

*devil-may-care: reckless and careless

flummox: to confuse

flush: a rush of stong feelings

full corned: drunk

go on the lift: steal

gruel: a thin, porridgelike soup

*hold a candle to the devil: someone as evil as the devil

ladybird: a prostitute

mad as hops: excitable

night walker: a prostitute

*pigeon-eyed: innocent

*pigeonhole: to label

*prigging: thieving

*round the clock: never stopping

sauce-box: a talkative mouth

*skilly: a thin broth of oatmeal and water

smasher: someone who passes bad money

smash-up: a battle to the end

sneak: thief

*sticky fingers: one with a tendency to steal

tart: a common girl with loose morals

*thick as thieves: close friends or coconspirators

toke: dry bread

tool: to pick a pocket

tosher: a sewer-hunter in the Victorian era

·· SOURCES ··

Main source: *Passing English of the Victorian Era* by James Redding Ware (George Routledge & Sons, Ltd., London, 1909)

OCT 2019